Yvette Walker is a Perth-based A
and bookseller. She is a graduat
Writing Program at Curtin Un
End of Love is her first novel.

UQP
LETTERS TO THE END OF LOVE
YVETTE WALKER

First published 2013 by University of Queensland Press
PO Box 6042, St Lucia Queensland 4067, Australia
www.uqp.com.au

Cover design by Allison Colpoys
Typeset in 12.5/15 pt Bembo by Post Pre-press Group, Brisbane
Printed in Australia by McPherson's Printing Group

National Library of Australia cataloguing-in-publication data
is available at http://catalogue.nla.gov.au

Letters to the End of Love / Yvette Walker
ISBN 978 0 7022 4966 2 (pbk)
978 0 7022 5101 6 (pdf)
978 0 7022 5102 3 (epub)
978 0 7022 5103 0 (kindle)

For M.F.R. – without whom a certain silent film star would still be selling gloves at Saks – Y.E.W.

He wrote often to Durham – long letters, trying carefully to express shades of feeling. Durham made little sense of them and said so. His replies were equally long. Maurice never let them out of his pocket, changing them from suit to suit and even pinning them in his pyjamas when he went to bed. He would wake up and touch them and, watching the reflections from the street lamp, remember how he used to be afraid as a little boy.

E.M. Forster, *Maurice*

June 1st 1969

Caithleen – This morning the notorious dog and I (once again) set off. Terns, cormorants and grey herons brought twigs of morning light through waning dark. The tide ran quicksilver, the fishing boats saluted the bay head. I smoked and I breathed but still barely used my Siberian lungs. I broke stones under my heavy boots. The dog woke as he walked. He yawned into still air, one ear up and then the other. The houses in St Joseph's Place slept. The Blessed Virgin prayed in her Grotto. As we escaped the village, the woodland's crown at our backs, the dog (once again) caught the scent of ducks: widgeon, tiny teal, mallard, and one, two Royal shelducks who have not left us for Germany. I whispered to the dog a small, simple sentence: 'No, my friend.' So he bowed his head. The tips of his ears quivered as he ceased his duck poetry. He is a good dog. At Mary O'Sullivan's cottage, there on her kitchen sill, a small lamp, taking in the light, giving the light out. The dog and I, we have taken this walk every morning now for this past year, yet every morning is unique, every morning breaks open like a fresh egg. As we walked I remembered the one last dream I had before waking. I dreamt I took a walk with a stranger's dog in a foreign country. Yudhishthira once did this, in the *Mahabharata*, when he walked with a found dog looking for the gates of Heaven. In my dream I didn't know if I was alive or dead. A cloak of nothing covered the birch wood I walked through. As I walked in my dream with an unknown dog I was afraid that Beckett was right – at the bottom of everything, nothing.

We came to the village bridge – no one there at all. We walked over its stone back, the curves of the estuary around us, and the ruins of the Abbey ahead. Our neighbours in Timoleague were sleepiness itself; the morning moved slowly in their bones, it lifted them awake and from their beds to the kettle and to the radio. The notorious dog sank lower the closer we came to the Abbey; his wolfhound gait as low as a thief. I coaxed him over the road. Celtic crosses correct as bishop's teeth shot up over the graveyard wall. The dog followed my shadow, but he refused (once again) to go any further than the gate so I walked into the Friary without him.

It isn't the headstones that frighten him (he cannot read them) it is the bones and the skulls he can smell turning in the earth. Deasy, O'Regan, Cahalane, McCarthy, O'Hea, and Kiely. Do you not believe, Caithleen, that a calcified Abbey is even Holier? When you can't sit or kneel or kiss the cloth, where you can but stand and look out to the water and the grey light sky beyond, then there is more, not less of God.

I have this evening (once again) fixed the old clock. I have read (once again) the Acmeist you left for me today. Of course, Akhmatova – 'He did not return, even after his death, to/That ancient city he was rooted in./Going away, he did not pause for breath/Nor look back. My song is for him.' I'm writing this in our bedroom, where the light is at its best. There is so much here that is ordinary. That you and I, we see every day. But that is what you want in these letters – Ordinary poetry. So . . . Our wedding rings rest on the bedside table. Around me your O'Donovan ancestors sleep in sepia. Your black Chanel on the back of the bedroom door and even after so many years, a faint fingerprint of Harlem cocaine there on the hem. A photograph, of a very young Paul Klee, smiles up at me from our dressing table, taken in his Weimar studio in 1922. On the wall above our bed, so beautiful is Klee's *Ad Marginem*. Last night, some time late last night I had a strange, deep dream about his painting. Now, in this morning (after my dream), it looks so different, but still so much the same as always. Let me explain. As always Klee's red sun surrounds delicate, tiny living things, small flowers that don't exist, flowers we've never seen in reality; and there, those strange, wrought shapes that are not one thing, not another. Our small duck stands, upside down as always, at the very top of the canvas. But this morning, Klee's sun, a floating red lantern, pulses below the duck and this morning I understand how life flourishes in the margins, regardless. And I remember the first time I saw the painting in our London hallway wrapped like a child for winter. I don't know what comes first, love or sadness, they are perfect twin pearls to me.

Caithleen, I am in love with Cork city's canals, the way that their thin white wrists stretch over the dark river Lee. Yesterday in the Huguenot Quarter, in your teashop, I watched you put your expensive Chinese tea away and I saw many old cinema tickets at the bottom of your shopping bag. And while you (once again) chatted on to the tea buyer I bought my first rock 'n' roll music. I saw, across the way in the window of another shop, a white record, copy after copy on display there. The notorious dog and I, we walked over and we went inside. And I asked the boy behind the counter for a copy of the record in the window. He looked at me, and asked if I was straight up. I said yes. He asked was it for my grandson or something like that and I said no, it was for me. He asked me why. I said I liked the cover (completely white with its own unique number, like a limited edition lithograph). The boy he laughed, he nodded and he laughed again. He put a copy of the record in a plain brown wrapper and wished me a good day granddad. And as I didn't tell you what I had bought, you would have assumed Shostakovich, or Bach. But no, not at all.

So this morning the dog and I took the white record into the old greenhouse, past the three shelves of empty vodka bottles, past the photographs of Claire, James, the Nieces (and their children), past my old suitcase full of papers, past my working canvas. This was when you were in your study. Were you chain-smoking through black market Edna O'Brien? Were you unpacking the boxes of draft paper that we bought at O'Leary's in Washington Street; enough paper to bind you to the novelist's curse until autumn? Were you sorting it out in the way that you like? I put the white record on top of the greenhouse radiogram. I have rewired the infernal machine (once again), but still it couldn't find Radio Éireann, still it only tuned in to the BBC's 'The Goon Show'. The dog stretched out on the floor like a Tatar prayer rug. I didn't know if I should do it to him. But I warmed up the player. I put on the first side of the first record. As the first song began (with the sound of a jet plane landing) the dog leapt up with a start and began to howl. I sat and smoked and listened. The dog put his head on my knee and looked up at me in bewilderment . . . Back. Back in November 1933, there were two men from the Secret Intelligence Service, dressed like salt and pepper shakers, there was a Black Maria, there was a long drive late into the countryside from London, there was a week of questions and questions and questions, there was no sleep, there was swearing, and the smashing of a blue china cup. Then, they let me go back to London, to have my press conference, but only because they were now so sure, so very damn sure I was cold and not hot – Russian, not Soviet.

I have never told you this. Or this:

Back. December 13th 1933, on the night we met. I walked through the lobby of my Bloomsbury hotel and into the bar, without footsteps. Behind me, three SIS men arrived and sat at separate tables, like the Holy Trinity, separate and together. I ignored them and went to the bar. I ordered my first vodka. Then in they came, the several men from the press, money and languages spilling from their suits. James slapped me on the back and in butchered Russian offered to buy my next drink.

I said no. Then I heard a woman's voice, which surprised me, and she said, 'Stop attacking the poor fella.' Claire. You said nothing, but smiled. I remember – you wore a beautiful wristwatch. Your lipstick was the colour of Massandra wine. And you were pale and a redhead, like a girl lost in a fairy tale, except you were a young woman. The other journalists, they took up with the SIS men, so we became alone at the bar – Claire, James, you, me. I don't know what you thought of me then – anything?

Today the rock 'n' roll made the notorious dog so very unhappy. The guitars were no louder than any Shostakovich symphony, but I could tell the dog would have much preferred an orchestra. His instincts glued him to the greenhouse floor, but his ears flicked back towards the door in some irritation. So I talked to him in the old language, not the modern dialectic, but in the poetry of Novosibirsk, my sparse cold words hiding warm lush language, and he replied to me in his lupine way, rolling the sounds around in his throat until they spilt out of the cage of his mouth; wet and sweet like birdsong. I had thought these musicians would be modern young men, but it was not so. There was retrospection. I didn't expect this. I listened to their lamenting guitars, and their simple, sentimental piano. I think, though I can't know it, that the dog liked the song about the weeping guitar – he stopped grinding his teeth while it played. I believe it could be my favourite as well. When the first side finished and I didn't change it over, the dog thumped his tail in happiness. I asked him to fetch the palette knife from the workbench. It was time for us to work.

My painting. I lifted one corner of my working canvas off the ground, and in an act of pure superstition, I shook it to settle the thousand shades of white I had placed there so many months before. Painting, it is the art of spies; it is a code that everyone can see but none can decipher. In this wall of canvas there was all white. The huge painting wanted so much to have colour but no, there would be only white; white guards on white horses in a Northern snowstorm, the very same, sad, old comedy. The dog nudged the palette knife into my hand, he walked the length of the canvas once, then lay down in front of the radiogram. The blood rushed to my hands, I shadow-boxed in front of the canvas, I lunged. It was not so difficult today. Rhythm invaded me and I cut new marks, chipped out old tracks of thought from the layers of white that walked down the centre of the painting, the white vertebrae I had constructed over months of work, a spine as thick as the trunk of a young pine tree. And I wished it were colder for me, so I could work better, but the painting, it needed all the warmth it could get, all the warmth I could gather in the old greenhouse, which after Michael's summer labour is now snug and warm. After an hour or so of paint, true to form, and on its own, the radiogram crackled to life (once again). The notorious dog shifted into a better listening position. 'The Last of the Smoking Seagoons' began. I took a step back from the painting to look. Strange signatures floated across the spine of the painting. In all the white, nothing was certain. Goons exploded in the air.

This painting, Caithleen, it began in my mind decades ago, began with Malevich. His brief rejection of colour was more than his Polish ego. The terror, Caithleen, the horror of no colour. But there is something. I paint white because I see white. That is what is left for me now in this world of cups and tea strainers, old magazines and vases of flowers, bowls of chocolate and wristwatches left on kitchen window sills.

While I was working you came out of the house. You, in your ill-fitting cardigan, a forgotten summer dress, expensive Spanish sandals, you looked beautiful to me. You cast an eye on my work. You asked me what bloody racket I had been listening to and I showed you the white cover. You laughed. You took the cigarette out of my mouth. You checked my heart as Dr Collins at Clonakilty showed you how. You brushed the cigarette ash from my shoulder.

I put my hands on your hips and you leant down to kiss me. The notorious dog approved.

In my deep, strange dream last night you and I walked along Nevsky Prospekt. We were walking home from *Stray Dog*. You questioned my choice of boots. They were provincial, not bohemian but peasant and you teased me. You said they were not Petropolis at all. That I should leave, go back to the North, find a tiny little Siberian village, find a single room with eighteen brothers and sisters and twenty pictures of The Boss on the walls. Not for love of him but to make the place a little warmer. I told you to go back to London, to afternoon tea and a parliament of secret communists and covert homosexuals. You said to me, 'They're not communists, Dmitri, they're socialists thank you very much. You may have the Party to contend with, but we still have the bloody English and their bloody Monarchy.' I didn't quite understand, but as I knew this was a dream (as you have never been to Russia) I forgave your insult. With an old key I found in my pocket I opened the door to the flat. You filled the pre-revolutionary brass samovar and I checked the stove. I opened the grate. Klee's sun had found its way inside. Its red rays shot out of the stove. They covered everything in a dark pomegranate light. Soon it was like living in a greenhouse. I took off my coat, my jumper, even my serf boots. You unravelled your scarf, you peeled off your coat. You sat at the table and began to type on Viktor's 1906 Odessa Underwood. Somehow you deciphered the Russian keys. I lit a cigarette and watched as strange plants sprang up from out of the ground. From out of nowhere they came. Unique botany never before seen, mischievous as jazz notes.

A duck with two red eyes wandered in from the kitchen and began to talk to me in English. 'My dear Dmitri Palovich,' he said to me, 'so glad you could come.' I asked if he would like a cigarette and he nodded. I placed one in his beak and I lit it for him. 'This is a beautiful painting,' he said to me, 'beautiful.' Yes, I saw. My entire flat was becoming the painting. Then I heard a bark, a familiar bark. I looked down at the street below to see the notorious dog barking up at me. I nodded for him to come and he ran up into the building. Minutes later he was scratching on the door. I let him in and he almost bowled me over. The glowing red sun made him nervous. He slunk under the table and curled up at your feet, growling every now and then. He didn't even try to chase the duck. Then the flat disappeared. The duck finished his cigarette, he dropped the butt from his beak and squashed it into the dirt with his webbed foot, then wandered off to look at a small, delicate red plant with four stems. You walked over to a thin plant that was at least ten feet tall. From one offshoot hung a bell-shaped flower the colour of mustard. The dog caught the scent of the duck and went off to find him. I told him he was only allowed to chase, not catch, and he grunted. You and I went walking. We wandered through the strange garden, through a breeze that picked up the dust and swirled it around our feet. We held hands, you pointed to all the different plants and I named them in Russian, English, Gaelic and Latin. Viktor walked through the dusty haze to greet us. He asked us if we had seen Krapp, Paul Klee's dog. We said no, but he could be with the notorious dog somewhere, chasing the duck perhaps? Viktor said that the duck was not a duck. I said I was sorry, I didn't realise this. For thirty years, I thought I was looking at a duck. It's a common mistake, Viktor said.

Yours, Dmitri.

June 6th 1969

Dmitri. Thank you. I have your letter, with its hand drawn stamp and postmark. You went to bed almost an hour ago now. The notorious dog refuses to sleep until I do. He lies across the doorway of the study like a Tibetan temple dog, sighing, hinting, perhaps, it would be best if I went to bed myself. But I have this to do first. You have written. If you were going to mock me, to make fun of my request for letters from my husband, you would have written to me in Russian, but there is nothing here except your cramped and slanted English, the words stacked up against one another like rows of roof tiles. The letter has everything I asked you for. I said I wanted ordinary things, ordinary poetry from you. So that is what you will get in return.

This morning, like every other morning, you drew a bath for me. Then you sat on the edge of our bed pulling on your boots, an unlit cigarette dangling from the corner of your mouth, your wedding ring on the bedside table beside mine. The dog bounded into the bedroom, banged straight into you and your cigarette fell from your lips, bounced off of him and landed on the carpet. You swore, picked up the cigarette and shoved it behind your ear. The dog tugged on your coat. I have seen this morning comedy for years now, but this morning it was to me illuminated somehow. Where the notorious dog came from who can say. Remember how he appeared one day, over four summers ago? – walking slowly up the long drive like a returned soldier. He had sand on his paws, as if he'd walked at low tide from Wood Point to the Pier. As if he'd jumped ship at Kinsale. I love the fact that he barks in

Russian even though he is an Irish wolfhound. And how we allow for his mysterious past. He has had a life we know nothing about, a history that is his to keep, and remember.

You waved one hand at me in that effortless goodbye: I first saw that wave nearly forty years ago. It could have been last night. I could have fallen in love with you yesterday. You left, taking with you your gruffness, the dog's enthusiasm. I heard you walking down the long drive, your steps fading out into the village road. I didn't want to get out of bed but thoughts about the novel had already begun. There was to be a party, at the main character's insistence, to celebrate his eighty-eighth birthday. It would be a disaster, of course. I got out of bed. I turned up the radio. I wrapped my red bathrobe around me. I took a packet of your cigarettes out of the bedside drawer and lit one. (Oh we know, dear one, I never let you smoke in the house.) I went into the bathroom with the cigarette and sat on the edge of the bath. I smoked and looked into the steaming water. I'd had a morning nightmare in which I was trying to run through a wood awash with mud while a murder pursued me; red-beaked choughs, grey crows, magpies and ravens. The dream was complicated and dark but I couldn't remember very much of it at all. I flicked the cigarette stub into the toilet and flushed it away to the sea. I tested the water with my elbow. It was cool enough so I slipped out of my bathrobe and into the bath. I didn't know how I was going to work today, my hands were locked up, my mind creased, my heart distracted. I closed my eyes, tilted my head back, and pushed the deepest part of the bath with my feet. Well, the night we met . . .

The night we met I thought it strange you weren't wearing a wristwatch. I didn't know then that there were no wristwatches in the Soviet Union. You had strong wrists and a painter's callus. You looked like you had lifted the world that morning and set it down again. What else? Your eyes were a strange blue I had never seen before, a blue I know now is only possible in Siberia, a blue that is burnt with white. And your fingernails were stained with nicotine. Your coat was beautiful, almost too elegant for you. I had to resist the urge to take your hands. You looked at me like a painter does, a world forming in your mind. Then you stopped. You held your hand out and introduced yourself. And so I found the truth.

In the bath I opened my eyes. I looked at my skin, the veins in my arm. I stood up carefully and stepped out of the water. I towelled myself off, put on my red bathrobe and returned to the bedroom. I sat on the bed, and, like you, looked at the photograph of Paul Klee, then up at the masterpiece he gave so generously, *Ad Marginem.* I see painted tapestry scattered with tiny creatures scrawled in dust and delicate lines. Klee's scrying sun allows everything else to live. I wondered if I would be able to look at it when you aren't here because it is a portrait of our marriage. I felt short, hot stabs of pain in my chest, like someone was unpicking my life from the inside. My arms and legs went weak and I felt dizzy. I lay back on the bed and tried to breathe. Death still frightens me the way he did when he first arrived, knocking at our back door like a salesman, his signature bold and flourished on your test results. I got up from the bed. I lit another cigarette. I dressed in a pair of favourite 1950s slacks, a new psychedelic t-shirt sent to me by one of the Nieces, and a store-bought blue cardigan from Dunnes that Granny would have hated. I went downstairs in search of tea.

You would be out for a few hours walking. After the diagnosis, Dr Collins at Clonakilty recommended walking to you, he also said you could keep up your painting. Well, I disagreed with him. I thought you should be resting but I knew there was no point thinking such things let alone suggesting them to you. You'd rather die out near One Cross with the dog than slumped in a chair or lying in a bed. This morning I looked out the kitchen window. The old light, the ancient light had come up from the bay, up over the coastguard cottages to us here on Granny's hill. It was playing its Song of the Earth. It made my eyes uncertain of the real (the house, the road, the greenhouse) and I begin to see strange things (the shadow of a raven, the tread of a fast horse, the red smudge of *Madra rua*). So I made tea, an Oolong from Guangdong province, long green shoots with chestnut highlights, a coppery amber tea, flowery and slightly bitter. I drank the Oolong slowly, I breathed, I drank, and my mind began to clear. I left the kitchen, taking my tea with me. I walked out of the back door and into the greenhouse. The enormous white painting was there, still in need of something, of many things. It made me think of Anne Madden's *Burren Land* even though she used a wider palette than white to conjure the light seeping into the limestone at Burren. But I could see how you both loved the palette knife; how you both loved to create a painting for contemplation.

As I looked at the white painting I finished my tea. I searched around for a pen, for a piece of paper. I knew which Acmeist to leave you today. Again, again, Akhmatova. I found a pen that worked, and a slightly grubby piece of drawing paper. I wrote down the complete poem. You would find it when you came in from your walk, weighted down by your palette knife. So obvious, I know, but I couldn't resist. Akhmatova, Mandelstam, Gumilev, they begin our days. It has always been this way. I wrote the poem, I left the poem, I went back to Granny's house. I think I left my tea cup on the greenhouse radiogram? I went upstairs to the study to begin my work.

I trace the map of other people's lives like an English cartographer, but I am not Virginia Woolf; no one in my fiction would buy flowers in that way. I continue to write the novel on my old workhorse, refusing the lure of newer, sexier typewriters. I dug into my work and I didn't even hear you come home. Later, I heard music coming from the greenhouse. The singer sang about a blackbird. And I remembered that when I woke from my dream this morning I felt very, very cold, as if I had flown a thousand miles with only a few feathers to shield me, and the taste in my mouth was metallic, bitter.

At a little after ten this morning Michael came up the long drive and delivered me my book, which he'd been told, under strict instructions, to deliver to my hands or not at all. When I heard his tread, the tyres of his bicycle, then the notorious dog's welcome bark, I knew you wouldn't bother at all to get up from your painting. The downstairs bell rang and rang and when I got to the door Michael was there, the notorious dog bouncing up and down beside him like an overwound top. 'Here is your American book,' Michael said (looking over my shoulder, to the cake I had baked, and the hot battered teapot) 'but you lost a ton of money on one little book, amn't I right?' I smiled, I smoothed the creases in the book's brown paper wrapping, I said, 'Same as that, Michael, same as that, won't you come in for tea.' And he said yes, same as he does every day, same as he has for over five years now, same as he did when we were summer visitors all those years. After our morning chat I thanked him, and I told him that the dog would see him out, down the drive, and into the village road. (Have a look, it's *Paul Klee's Diaries*, 1898–1918.)

Dmitri. You only believe in three things, Klee, the notorious dog, and me. If I had a thousand years I would need each of them to talk about you, one year for each of your personalities, but without that expanse of time it is too daunting to speak, you are too big, too complicated. Words don't work. Your heart is trying to burst out of your body, it's been trying for forty years. I'd like to say I have protected you, but you were never the kind of man who needed anyone's protection. Your heart is folding into itself like a collapsing tent. I am too numb to be angry. I suppose the anger will come once you are gone. I can't imagine. I am supposed to prepare myself for this after, for years of after. It's not as though I don't wish to be alone, some days.

Especially when you are overbearing and relentless, your Siberian shadow everywhere, all over Granny's house. But no, not this final goodbye. My love for you is shifting, archiving, preparing to become a memory. Your heart has its own syncopation. You told me once that when you were sixteen, your heart had fallen. Tonight, you are deep in dreams, your heart held in its cavity like a sleeping drunk in a yawl, rocking in the low tide of the bay.

The dog is nudging me. The night is getting older, the long spring light is dying and the cold blue dark is pouring into the yard, making the house a little uncomfortable. The dog has begun to be a little worried about you and I. There are fine lines beginning to form at the edges of his eyes, wisps of grey swirl into the backs of his ears and although it is well understood he loves you the best, his care and attention for me has reached new heights. He suspects something difficult is coming.

Caithleen.

19/09/2011

Hey Lou –

Very late last night, Nate smoked under our pomegranate tree. He drew the smoke close to his body, not wanting to let it go. He savoured the cigarette with such style, I almost believed it was good for him, you know? There was no guilt, or hint of addiction, only charm and romance, something from the early twentieth century. All his friends had gone home, it was around four in the morning. Pete picked up empty beer bottles from under the Chinese elm and sang,

Just like an old time telegraph man,
I came here with a simple job to do.

I sat on the steps with a sleepy Crow Bait in my arms. Despite all the noise Crow Bait had been dozing most of the night, dear old tabby. Pete stood on the concrete path, stretched and yawned, then eased his head back to look at the Southern stars. 'You won't be seeing those for a while,' he said to Nate. Nate stubbed his cigarette out in your ancient Waltham Abbey ashtray. A second later he lit another, reached up into the tree and plucked a perfect pomegranate, one of the few not overripe and exploded. Ah, the fruit of the underworld. Nate brought the pomegranate over to show his father and me. He shook it like a Goon Show bomb and said, 'How do you get the seeds out, Aunty Grace?' So, I told him what you told me all those years ago – that you cut the fruit in half, hold one half over a bowl, with the cut side cupped in your palm. I pictured you using the back of a wooden spoon to gently knock the pomegranate skin, how the seeds came out naturally and fell through your fingers. He flicked ash from his cigarette into the bamboo by the steps, shoved the smoke into the corner of his mouth and sidestepped his way into the house. I called after him, 'Catch the juices in the bowl or they'll go everywhere, Nate!' His reply was a hearty 'Righto, Aunty Grace!'

Pete sat down on the steps beside me. I handed him Crow Bait and he slung the cat over his shoulder. I asked Pete if Nate had registered his trip with Foreign Affairs. Pete said yes but he'd had to bribe Nate to do it. This had cost Pete five hundred US dollars. And Pete was now on Facebook – well, to be more accurate, Crow Bait was now on Facebook (did you know that our cat's favourite movie is *Butch Cassidy and the Sundance Kid*?). I said Nate had asked me to go on Facebook too but I told him send me postcards. Pete tweaked Crow Bait's ears. 'You've got Buckley's of that happening,' he said to me. And Nate was worried about the pianist that had been arranged for him in New York. I said to Pete, Nate would be holding out to find some eighty-year-old guy who had worked with Friedrich Hollaender. You know that Nate first heard cabaret in this backyard but I've never told you the whole story. It was about two years before you and I met. Pete had come over with Nate to have dinner. Patrick was on his way up from St George's Terrace. Eight-year-old Nate lay on his back in the grass (a kittenish Crow Bait curled up on his chest) and listened for the first time to Kurt Weill. And as I watched Nate lying in the grass that night enraptured with those sounds, I thought the boy's body would burst into blossom. And years and years later, that night I took him to see Ute Lemper when he was seventeen (you were away somewhere) he said to me afterwards that it was the best two hours of his life. I remember that he lounged in the kitchen doorway and mimicked what Ute had said that night, 'This is a song about a city that never sleeps . . . Not like . . . Perth.'

Last night Nate called to Pete and I from the kitchen, 'It's working!' and Pete yelled, 'Well, bring the bloody bowl out here then!' Nate grumbled something inaudible. 'And beer!' Nate came out with three cold Black Swans and a white bowl of pomegranate seeds. He sat between his father and me, still smoking in his effortless way. I looked at Nate and it seemed that he wasn't like all the other Whitlock men, men with the bodies of surfers or shearers who ended up being journos or CPAs (though Nate's voice, his voice is that of his grandfather and his great grandfather, rough and sweet, you know?) Tall, lithe Nate, with a profile only seen in old movies – it was plain to me that he was becoming so much like the men on his mother's side. Even though they disappeared from his life before he could walk, there they were on our back steps, the generations before him. By the time he was ten it was clear that Nate would not be stocky like his father but a tall bugger, with a perfect build for football. 'Proper football,' Pete would say to me then, 'not that bloody meat locker game they love over east.' And you remember, all the years of junior football, then National Under 18s, then colts, until at eighteen he hung up his boots and wouldn't say a bloody word about it, not to us, not to his dad. It's easy to see why now. Bloody hell. Didn't Nate's coming out blow our idea of him out of the water?

Didn't we feel like idiots for not knowing? It seems a lifetime ago now, now Nate has shrugged off his shyness and stumbled into his adulthood with bravado and naivety. How he has changed. He is so much more himself. Now, all of a sudden, here he was, about to fly into the world in that effortless way the young have, all forward motion, fly away from Perth to perform his Paul O'Montis songs in Brooklyn. I was so proud, watching him perform in the Spiegeltent at Perth Fringe this year, singing into the same air as Dietrich and Chaplin. So last night Nate, Pete and I sat on the back steps and ate pomegranate seeds. We raised our beers to Nate's journey and blessed him.

Some afternoons I'm hanging around my inbox like a kid waiting outside school for her sweetheart. But I wanted to give you something else while you are out there in the world, you know? Something to do with memories, recent and past, something to do with the way language can record the world and give intimacy back to you through its slow and steady pulse. I want you to remember.

Nate's tenth birthday, the day we met, a memory like a movie. You came through the door with Nate's friend Tim, in a little black dress with a turquoise scarf, petite silver earrings, short dark hair a bit wet from the rain. You laughed at something Nate said and I could barely keep my eyes off of you. Someone said you were Tim's aunty roped in at the last moment when his mother realised she had double-booked herself. Later that rainy Saturday afternoon, it was our job to cut and plate up the ice-cream cake. I felt dizzy, and couldn't stop looking at your hands. I remember saying idiotic things, which you replied to with skill and diplomacy. Who knew if you were gay, who knew if you were straight, I couldn't tell, I've never been any good at telling such things. My secret plan was to stop you leaving the house. Or to follow you when you left. Or to interrogate Nate and find out where Tim lived, so I could pop in some time and bring the conversation around to you – ridiculous, stupid plans that would come to nothing.

As the afternoon wore down, so did my resolve. By the time I was doing the dishes (while Pete was wrestling a dozen ten-year-old boys in a vain attempt to burn off all the sugar they had imbibed that day), I had given up on ever seeing you again. Then Pete emerged roaring from the mountain of giggling boys, and you appeared at my side, tea towel in hand, and began speak. Every dried dish revealed a small truth. You confessed: you had asked your sister if you could bring Tim to Nate's party. You'd seen me one day outside the school walking Nate home. You knew I couldn't be his mum. You had your sister ask Pete about me, discreetly of course, in case you'd got the wrong end of the stick. Apparently, you were bad at picking these things too. You looked at me and smiled. And I was so impressed. Your plan to meet me, it was simple, it was elegant, it was Jane Austen in its execution. Remember?

Please say you remember. Because underneath all these years together, is that original happiness, the look of recognition on your face that afternoon, the possibility of joy.

I understand that things have been difficult for a long time now, like we have been trudging through mud, getting somewhere but not a whole lot of somewhere, and we both feel tired, bone tired, and irritated by the things we need to do to keep this hand-built life ticking over, and we are not very happy. I don't know. I could blame your constant travelling for work, as I have late at night when you are in no state to argue with me and I know I can have a good lunge at you; you could blame my cowardice, if that is what it is, my general disinterest in anything beyond my family, my house and my tiny bookshop. We'd both be right, in many ways, we'd both have a strong argument, and still things would not be better, we would not be better. So I'm trying something here, something old fashioned, something possibly redundant in a world of speed and light, but I don't know what else to do, and you aren't here.

When you go away, something happens to my dreams; as if your leaving opens up a complex series of tunnels, tracks and archways, which I must journey along, alone in the dark. Last night I dreamt we were living together in Saint-Germain des Près. (Today I thought, Paris, but of course, the perfect cliché for cuckoldry.) Along our lounge room wall ran a floor-to-ceiling bookcase crammed with French novels. I was wrestling with a Sony Walkman that was wound around my neck and my head. Behind me were cities of stereo equipment. Kristin Scott Thomas was sitting on our white couch. You entered the room carrying a chair. Kristin smiled. I felt like an idiot, as I couldn't get the bloody Walkman off. You shed your cardigan, draped it over the back of the chair. You then took off your blouse and began talking in French to Kristin. She lit a cigarette and asked me in English if I wanted one. I declined. She walked over to the bookcase, pulled out a volume at random and began to flick through it. I charged out of the lounge, down the long white hallway and into our bedroom. You were changing into a black Dior, putting on Chanel No.5. I finally pulled the Walkman free and hurled it to the floor. Suddenly we were standing in the open closet – you with your back to the wall; me half an inch from your nose shouting, 'What is this? What does this mean?' And you shrug – smiled at me in that infuriating Parisian way and said, 'This is the wrecking ball.' I woke up, my heart twisted and grotesque, my throat sore with the taste of burnt chicory, the taste of betrayal.

It's because I don't know where you are. As soon as I picture you in one place, you are gone again, onto another plane, to another city, another hotel, your BlackBerry as faithful as Ulysses' dog. It's because the world is full of women not only more interesting than me, but far more dangerous than that, women who are more sophisticated, more worldly, how could they not be, look where they are, out in the world, with you. And I sit at home in Perth waiting, like Penelope minus the suitors, tapestries unravelling, like I have for years now.

Since you've been gone, it's taken a little bit of time to move beyond the sheer relief of being alone, without all that hard work between us, the wrestling we do. So it's hard to describe this feeling of loneliness I have, strung out like washing for all to see. It's a little like fainting, a little like the feeling you get just before you are going to be ill, a little like vertigo, you know? It surprised me. It's not as if you being away is something unusual. Getting on airplanes is like getting on buses for you, it's such a normal part of life. Nothing has changed since you have been away, there have been no miracles. Is it over six years now since I have been on a plane?

Not even to Melbourne, or Sydney. This summer, since you've been gone, I've been taking long bus rides to country towns – York, Northam, Toodyay. These bus rides have confirmed what I've been thinking since I stopped flying – that you miss out on so much if you fly over everything. The logic of the land, the messages of the country are lost to you up there. There's no poetry in modern flight, you know? Only speed. In the past six years I have fallen in love with real time, the way light arrives and falls through the world.

This morning I dragged out that Paul Klee print Patrick left me and put it up on the kitchen wall, where the light is the best. I had a cup of tea and took a good look at it. Patrick could in no way be called an art lover, but I remember a tatty version of this particular painting had been stuck to the wall above his desk all the way through university. God how he loved the duck, the red sun, and the funny botanical characters lurking at the bottom of the painting like an animator's drunk. He'd ripped that first copy out of one of the folio-sized art books in the Murdoch University library. Pete was always threatening to dob him in but never would have. All through his uni years Patrick never thought he would get to see the real thing, but he did in the end, and more than once. Any time he found himself in Europe, he would try to swing a flight to Basel somehow, and if he succeeded he'd walk to the Kunstmuseum from the train station and sit in front of *Ad Marginem*. I found out recently – did I tell you? – that Paul Klee had given *Ad Marginem* away as a wedding gift to a fellow painter in the 1930s – and fifty years later the painting was given back to his son Felix, which is how it returned to Switzerland! Lou, I still see Patrick. He walks the streets of Perth, whistling, on his way to nowhere in particular, maybe up Murray Street to the Melbourne Hotel for a beer, maybe to 78 Records to find that elusive Triffids album, maybe down to the stock exchange on the Terrace to sniff out one last story for the week. Patrick walks through that late afternoon light which brushes the lamp-posts and the parking meters, good honest light that washes away the speculations, the ligations, and the accusations of the CBD. Beer is in the air, the first beer of the end of the day, the anticipated pleasure of gossip, stirring and taking the piss. Patrick has wrenched his tie, loosed his bloody awful tie, one of the ones Dad gave him when he first graduated, a decade ago. He's happy, and thirsty, ready to prop up a bar and tell a story. Patrick walks in Perth.

Pete and I took Nate to the airport this morning. Pete joked that the departure lounge had been opened especially for Nate – no one else seemed to be around. The café windows afforded us that view of the city you love, where Perth looks like the Emerald City in *The Wizard of Oz*, a small cluster of cardboard skyscrapers stuck in the middle of wide-open land. Pete and I played a game of Fast Scrabble while Nate checked, checked and rechecked his smartphone. Nate's open leather satchel spilled out a grey Leuchtturm 1917 notebook, several black Artline 5.0s, his tattered biography of Paul O'Montis, and, like something out of film noir, a sizeable wad of US dollars. And on Nate's wrist, his uncle Patrick's watch moved forward, forward. All my love, Grace.

30th September 2011

Grace. First-class passengers sleep while the heavens slip under the blinds. I can see Stow's small black tattoo (the initials LR) under the first knuckle of his right thumb. A well-cut glass of Jameson's slumbers on his tray table, flakes of tobacco remain on his Sheplar's jacket. Stow drinks his whisky and reads *Vagabond Holes*, while I sip Lady Grey tea. Women in business class are sending him *billet doux*. I don't stop their notes coming but they don't get any further than me. I want to tell you I don't read these little love poems but of course I do (what a well-educated woman can suggest to a complete stranger in a little under six sentences . . .). Poor Stow. Now he's been proclaimed the new Dylan, he can't flick a chocolate bar wrapper into a New York wastepaper basket without causing a riot. And since he's married Lucy, the women of the world just want him more, but they never turn his head (I am yet to work that one out). Since your letter I've been thinking about the first time I saw you. You were coming out of Mt Lawley Primary with Nate, both of you laughing at something, and I looked your way. Something happened in me. I almost dismissed it but I remember saying to myself don't make the mistake of thinking oh, it's nothing, you don't know that it's nothing. Yes, I concocted that ridiculous excuse to come to Nate's birthday party. Did I say I felt a little ashamed? – but I did it anyway. As soon as I saw you again that day I knew I had done the right thing. Yesterday evening in Los Angeles the young man behind the reception desk gave me your letter. How unexpected. I've recalled that when we were first together you said to me, 'Let's write letters to one another, you know, like the famous blue raincoat.' And that we did, but not for long I think (was it because the whole world went online – is that why we never wrote another word?). I opened your letter immediately. When I began to read there was Nate, smoking under the pomegranate tree, and there was Pete, collecting empties, and there you were, sitting on our back step with Crow Bait in your arms, telling Nate how to remove pomegranate seeds just as I told you all those years ago. And I was at home. I could see early morning light bursting through the pomegranate tree, setting alight its red tips. I love your emails but this letter of yours, it breathes. I'd forgotten that letters could do that. They are so corporeal. It makes me realise that there's no depth in data, it's purely for pleasure, candy really. But Grace, what am I doing in Paris making love to Kristin Scott Thomas? Out here in the world, I am too tired, too distracted, too busy to look at other women. Not so long ago, sex with you was as natural as breathing. I don't know what happened. After I read your letter I thought about one night a few years ago now, one night when we were alone at home and we danced to Gillian Welch, just for a little while, and I felt in love and good and alright. I know you are worried for Nate but it's a migratory thing, when you're born and bred in Perth you have to leave. And *Ad Marginem*. Paul Klee's duck. Yes, I know, Patrick told me how he went back many times to see the real thing. He told me of his flights and flights to Basel (so Patrick). I see Patrick every time I hear Pete laugh; or when Nate keeps hammering away at the same damn point, no matter if he is actually right or wrong. I remember at Patrick's memorial service, watching you. And those weeks before, always watching you. In case you were going to break, or fall apart and not come together again. You never did fall, but now I wonder if I only saw what I needed to see. I think I will join Stow in his whisky. It should be remarkable that you can fly over the top of the world, but for the majority of us it is only one more thing to get through. Stow's wedding band is very plain white gold. There are words inscribed. I wonder what it's like, to wear a wedding ring. Would you forget it was there, would it mean anything after years? I've imagined marrying you many times. Being the organiser that I am I have fantasised about every little detail. On really difficult trips it became a way to relax, to get away from the unrelenting schedule of work. In my mind, we've been married oh at least fifty times. But recently I haven't thought about it. So, there is no getting around it. I don't want to delay a conversation about us any longer; and I gather that you don't either. Your idea of letters, I think it's a good one. I suppose it's natural, you see the world through language. I'll try to give you what you need, but you have to know from the beginning that I am so pressed for time that you'll never get a very long letter. I'm afraid they'll be written fast; whispered against whatever wall I've crashed into after a long day with Stow. You know me, Grace. I work in systems, strategies, probabilities, politics. I predict disaster, I manage unknowns, I keep things on track. Work things, but not you and I. I might fail at this. This is a different mode altogether. No one does this any more (except for the articulate ladies in business class so enamoured with celebrity they can't help but press little love letters into the palms of the passing cabin crew). Love letters. That's what we'll write. Not romance, not porn, but letters that talk about love as it is, in all of its strangeness. Love, Lou.

June 1st '48

Dearest David,

If you hadn't smoked, and I hadn't looked like a man who had a spectacular gift for telling the time, we never would have met. Or perhaps it was the uniform that attracted you, the white coat, the stethoscope. On July 21st 1929, you were smoking on the stairs of Barts, a newspaper tucked under your arm like a dispatch from a war room. Your hat was pulled down over your face and you were flicking the cigarette ash across your body as if it were incense. I was escorting the distressed husband of a patient down the stairs, reassuring him that his wife would come through this difficult period. I was deliberately speaking to him in tones that would calm him, tones I'd practised and perfected. By the time I got him to the bottom of the stairs the slight tremor in his left hand had stopped and he could look me in the eye. He thanked me, shook my hand, and told me he would be back tomorrow with the children. I said that would be wonderful, his wife would like that and he smiled, briefly, before walking away from me and out the entrance. I stood there for a moment, reviewing his wife's case in my mind and tapping my chest with my stethoscope, looking for a way into her condition that I couldn't see yet, but that I knew would come with time. I turned to go back up the stairs and I noticed you again. You had taken your hat off, though the cigarette was still burning in your left hand. The newspaper threatened to fall out from under your arm and you had the most spectacular blue eyes. You were surprised by something. You noticed my watch and asked me for the time. Perhaps love at first sight is a ridiculous notion, encouraged in bestsellers and popular songs, perhaps it isn't. I can't say it was love with you, definitely not at first sight, perhaps curiosity is the better word. You were beautiful, but I was not, in my doctor's coat and shoes, about to kiss you on the stairs of Barts. I had kissed men of course, long before I met you, I had sex with them on occasion, on many occasions, but I was not about to with you. You looked like you weren't allowed to cross the road without permission.

Tennis seemed an appropriate offer. You said yes, but you would need to borrow clothes from my wardrobe. You were quite good actually. From the first, Vivienne was very taken with you, even though she knew quite well why I invited you and why you accepted. She liked to charm any young man she could, just for the practice. Walking in my grandmother's West Cliff garden with Vivienne, you told her about the cottage your family had in Sulz, how you would take her there and the two of you would go walking in the Vienna Woods. You explained to Viv that your father lived in Berlin, your mother in Vienna. It was an arrangement that suited them both. Vivienne laughed, and remarked on the strange, physical laws inherent in marriage, which, after many years of shared intimacy, flung the husband and wife out into separate spheres. She took your arm and told you how Father spent most of his time here in the Red Villa, our West Cliff house, while Mother lived for the most part (with me) at Crawford House, the Richmond address. When you asked why the Red Villa, why not the Red House, Viv told you the story of Lillie Langtry.

I have your triptych of paintings called *Metropole* depicting a fragmented Vienna. The Ringstrasse is being torn up by a train full of light that is crashing through buildings, cars and pedestrians. My darling, you painted these gigantic canvases in our tiny apartment in the Rummelhardtgasse, it took you almost all of '31. You painted while the Viennese continued to go in droves to Lehar's *Die lustige Witwe*, desperately inoculating themselves against a future without cure. I also have, from '32 and '33, *Kussen 1*, *Kussen 2*, *Kussen 3*, *Kussen 4*, but *Kussen 5* and *Kussen 6* are missing. These I understand. We would kiss in the early morning before I went to the university to teach. During our first months in Vienna you only let me speak to you in German, so by the time I took up my post, I could at least hold a reasonable (if overly formal) conversation about breakfast, bread rolls and the Social Democrats. In that first year in Vienna you made me lie in bed with you and tell you stories about my childhood, all English banned from the bed, and I would talk about when my father taught me to dive, how my first, perfect dive made him look at me in a way he had never looked at me before, with admiration, and pride. I told you I had strange, small boy's memories of my mother singing Schubert to me, but by the time I was six she had been mysteriously replaced by someone unrecognisable, a woman with a sternness I hadn't noticed growing over her heart until it was too late. I also have your paintings of the Potsdamer Platz, the ones that have splatters of your own blood interspersed with brown, grey and blue paint, the result of getting too close to a policeman's truncheon. Forgive me, you know I am still trying to understand many of your paintings. I try to see what it is you were seeing but I am still too linear, too logical, some days all I can see is they don't look like the world. But as my heart becomes more fragmented, dissected, unstable, I am able to understand them a little bit more. As I begin to understand that what I look like (a man intact) and what I experience (a man collapsing into himself) can both exist at once, I begin to see your work more clearly from a wounded eye.

I have writing paper, my father's whisky, and spiv cigarettes hidden in a false drawer in my writing desk (for the day I have to take them up again). I have the ghost of you pressing against my ribs like deep water. It is only now, in this cardigan of a house that I begin to miss you, and to grieve. Since the end of the war, Vivienne has travelled to Bournemouth from Richmond every weekend to check on every little thing, the hydrangeas in the garden, the rationed loaves of bread, the position of the sun in relation to the earth. Now Vivienne has come to spend the summer with me, she has stepped up her Sam Vickers campaign. I find his card around the Red Villa, little talisman of sanity left on the hall table, in the kitchen drawers, on the mantelpiece. I collect these cards religiously, late in the evening, hours after she has turned in, then burn them, one by one, the ashes collapsing into grandmother's ashtray. I find this little ritual incredibly cathartic, much more effective than actually calling Vickers. Viv brings in flowers every third day from the garden, and places them strategically throughout the house, making me feel like the featured corpse at the funeral parlour. She interrogates Mrs Halligan, drilling her about my eating habits, my drinking habits, my nightmares. Vivienne assumes I have nightmares, which I do, but I will never speak of them. You have probably guessed that I also dream of you –

In last night's dream we were at a party and you were telling a joke about Goering, Marlene Dietrich and Himmler. Waiters walked the room, offering empty silver trays to the guests that they politely refused. I watched you chat to Carter and Lawrence, you laughed so hard at your own joke they joined in out of love for you. I smoked and I watched you, strung up in my black tie. I looked (to all the world) like a respectable gentlemen. I checked my watch and it was a quarter to midnight. You caught my eye and smiled at me through the haze of smoke, your blue eyes suggesting all manner of things that I shan't go into here. You had loosened off your tie and popped the top two buttons on your dress shirt. You began to walk over to me and I could just make out your Adam's apple, and the fact you had cut yourself shaving that morning. That was my fault. I had come up behind you and kissed your right shoulder blade, making you nick yourself. Someone put Strauss on the gramophone and you asked me to dance. We took to the floor like an old married couple and I asked you what Heaven was like. Crowded, you said. It is almost impossible to get a good table for dinner. Heaven, you said as we danced, was a Grand Hotel full of frustrated people with complaints for God. You were placated with beautiful furniture and beautiful angels. And you smoked of course. Those Turkish cigarettes you loved. You had imagined Heaven to be full of light, like some Impressionist paradise, but it wasn't like that at all. The day whimpered like a light bulb too weak for a large room. Every night in the dining room you looked for someone you loved, but Heaven was a country of strangers. You walked alone, at night, through the corridors of the Grand Hotel when the rest of the dead were asleep and you listened to their dreams. You passed angels in the corridors and they placed their tapered fingers to their perfect lips. You nodded, and listened to the sleep talk coming from every room. Some dreamt of their children. They talked to them as if they were on the telephone. Some dreamt of their murderers. They screamed out to them, enraged. Some dreamt of their husbands, their wives, their lovers. They whispered sweet nothings to them, as if they were lying beside them, so close. You wandered the corridors and waited for me to dream of you. Sometimes I would dance with you, share a joke, a conversation. Then we would part.

I am surrounded by your paintings, they fill every room, competing with Vivienne's flowers. Before VE Day I had all of your paintings stored away upstairs, meticulously labelled and catalogued. But after the end of the war in Europe, and your mother's letters, memories of you began to seep into everything, they mingled with the 9 o'clock BBC news, Vivienne's *Picture Post* stories, Mrs Halligan's shopping lists, my doctors' strict instructions taped on the back of my bedroom door. So I began to bring your paintings downstairs. Your mother is still sending me canvas, she wants me to have everything you ever did, your student work, your sketches, catalogues from your exhibitions, photographs of you standing in front of your favourite paintings, she wants me to have all of you. The post is filled with regret and remorse. I don't keep a single photograph of you, of anyone, on display in the Red Villa. This alone has convinced Vivienne I need analysis from Sam Vickers. It isn't the daily drinking, or the anxiety, or the fact I look like a bloody undertaker, all skin and bone. No, according to Vivienne, I need analysis because I have no pictures of Mother or Father, or of her at Lady Margaret Hall, or Alistair's wedding day, or any of my tennis matches. I do have one photograph that I keep in the bottom drawer of my bedroom chest. It's wrapped in my tennis jumper. In the photograph you're alone in the garden sitting on an old, white, wrought-iron chair surrounded by the tropical plants my grandmother had put in just before the First War, great South American things with cooling green leaves the size of platters. Your back is jammed up against the back of the chair, your feet are resting on a small tea chest and you are smoking. Your cigarette is in your left hand, which is resting on your thigh. You're careful not to flick ash on your tennis trousers – mine, you had to borrow them to play that first afternoon as you had none of your own. You are spinning a tennis racquet on its head, by flicking the handle with the thumb and two fingers of your right hand. You are not looking at the camera, you are looking out into the space where the tennis court would be. You're thinking that you'd much rather be back in Berlin, painting, than playing tennis in Bournemouth with people you hardly know, but there is me, and I am strangely compelling. Vivienne took this photograph of you but I can tell by your studied casualness that you knew it would be given to me.

Mrs Halligan is in the kitchen doing the washing up. I offered to help but she gave me such a look I bade a hasty retreat. The sun is pushing through the mid-morning gloom like Leslie Howard through a

London crowd. Vivienne's fled down the Zig Zag, along West Cliff Prom to the Pier Approach Baths to do her lengths. When she returns, she'll insist I get up and go for a walk, whatever the weather, have a cup of tea, something useful. Not just collapse on the sitting room settee and stare at the ceiling, looking at the universe in an R.W. Edis inlay. She doesn't seem to understand there is nothing left to fall apart. I'm like a man who continues to live in his house once the walls have collapsed. Which would be funny if I were Keaton, or Chaplin; ironic if I were Kafka or Brecht, but I'm just a doctor with no sense of humour. This was something you always appreciated about me. You found it refreshing that I didn't try to be clever, I didn't even try to make you laugh. I just offered to tell you the time. In my old working life before we met, I'd glance at my watch at half past five in the morning, every morning, and travel to Barts. I could be relied upon to be back at Crawford House at a quarter to seven in the evening, weather and trains permitting. I would then be available for regular updates on the time and the occasional conversation until a quarter to eleven, when, more often than not, I would go to bed.

Some nights I wake up with a violent start, my heart in a frenzy, and I believe that I am dead, that I have woken up from life and I'm lying in some celestial waiting room. Then I hear your Longines ticking on the nightstand, and I know with sickening absolute truth that I am still alive, moving forward in time, leaving you behind. Making love with you is when I first began disbelieving in time, in the argument that the quality of time is uniform, that it is always the same, from one second to the next. That wasn't my experience with you. I began to disbelieve my wristwatch, to doubt my ability as a timekeeper. Time with you had its own logic, a painter's logic, it seems to me now. You'd walk around me like I was a canvas to contemplate, you'd select your way of approaching me then apply the right colour and line to my heart, slowly, selectively, until you could do no more, for now. Through you I understood the soul of the artist. Before you, I thought such a thing was a stereotype, an act, merely a way of seeking attention and publicity. Now I know it is a completely unique way of being, your gentle, studious nature not weakness but flexibility, the strongest defence against anything – the ability to see something in a thousand different ways.

I don't have that ability. I never did. I am as unambiguous as an x-ray. Compassion I could manifest. I used imagination to think my way to the solution to all sorts of medical problems, but I have a problem with sight. Hence my inability to see your paintings. I don't understand what it is that you are seeing. Not yet. I'm trying, as I told you before, it's important you understand that. I am trying. I spend many of my weekend hours studying your work, then cracking open a small book on the work of Paul Klee, which Vivienne gave me last year; trying to see him in you. Your vision of the world was multi-dimensional, multi-layered; mine was linear, logical, ordered and English. I struggle with the abstract. The irony of pastiche I understand, but the pure emotional painting is still something that is beyond me. As much as I love you I still don't fully understand you. I thought I had a lifetime to try.

John.

June 3rd '48

Dearest David,

Vivienne can see my slow unravelling, but she refuses to lose faith in a happier year, when she will have me back again. Alistair is still climbing the monkey bars of the Conservative Party. All I see of him is a striding black coat in Beaverbrook's *Evening Standard*; his dull, journeyman speeches quoted in the *Spectator*, the *Daily Telegraph*. This morning on the beach Viv took my arm like she used to take yours. We talked of her visits to Vienna in the early thirties, when she'd telephone our place to speak to you. You'd spend an hour talking to her, gossiping, then hang up without letting me speak to her, and announce that Fräulein Carpenter was en route and you had to quickly, quickly line up as many beautiful men as possible (not something you found difficult to do). I asked Viv if she remembered the Kabarett singer from Berlin who was so smitten by her, she said that she remembered he was so very tall, 'even taller than you, Johnny' and very funny.

In our apartment in Vienna that day, where there was champagne, and boys, the Kabarett singer Kurt Ehrlich dedicated a song to Vivienne, Claire Waldoff's 'Raus mit den Männern'. Kurt had telephoned you after he moved to Vienna. People heard he was coming to our apartment and soon the place was packed with Berliners, Viennese and our Vivienne. Vivienne helped you engage your brilliant drinks system. She wandered through the crowded room encouraging the young men to pass their empty glasses back towards the kitchen. When the empty glasses came back to you standing in the kitchen doorway you filled them with chilled champagne and sent them out again. I was the iceman. My job was to break up the ice, roll it into the kitchen sink and make sure the champagne was kept cold. I remember Kurt twisted the cork out of a bottle slowly like a Parisian waiter and poured the overflowing champagne into seven champagne glasses he had lined up along the floor like footlights. The world fitted Kurt like an outgrown jacket. He was as graceful as a dancer, with a mellow, modern voice, like that of a Harlem Negro. That day, Kurt also sang Hollaender's 'Münchhausen'. The legendary baron did what he does best, lied through his teeth, talking of a brave republic flying its stripes of black and red and gold, and gone are those flags which sport that thing that zigs and zags. I told Vivienne this morning on Durley Chine that Kurt had written to me after the war. He had survived internment. He had performed in entertainment revues which where staged at Westerbork; he had performed in the same hall where new inmates were processed, in the same hall where his fellow Jews went to apply for exemption from deportation to the East.

On our way back up to the West Cliff, Viv and I talked about Mother, her love of Beethoven above all of us. Vivienne and I could never imagine her without Beethoven. When we were small he was like the older, smarter, more favoured brother, even more loved than Alistair, and we couldn't compete with him. I told Viv I used to lie in bed when I was quite small, thinking of ways I could get to Germany so I could have it out with Herr Beethoven. I had to stop him sending his scores, his recordings to Mother. I thought I could hide in a mailbag. When the mail went to Southampton on the train I would be with it. I could empty out the letters on the way. Then I would carry the bag to the nearest seaman's den (they were everywhere in Southampton). I would eavesdrop on the conversations of the sailors, and find out who was heading for Germany. Then I would crawl into my mailbag and a sailor on his way to Germany would mistake the bag for his duffle and carry it to his ship. I knew if I got to Germany it would be easy to find Herr Beethoven's house, because everyone in Germany knew Herr Beethoven. I imagined myself marching right up to his house and knocking on his door. When he opened the door, he would know who I was and why I was there. There would be an almighty brawl between Beethoven and I, right in his front garden, in front of his neighbours and the passers-by. Even though he was much older than me (I was six, he was in my mind very old, almost nineteen), I would be driven by the urgency of my mission and he would be no match for that. After my final blow, he would collapse in the garden, sobbing, and promise never to send Mother any music ever again, not one sheet, not one gramophone record. Mother would be sad for a little while, that was normal, but soon she would realise she now had so much more time to be with Vivienne, Alistair and I.

Vivienne laughed. She said she was happy to be back at the Red Villa, she missed the old place, but she had the City now, her work at the *Picture Post*, and there was the Chap. I asked how the Chap was and she said extraordinary. One marriage had been enough for her though, and they were too old for such nonsense. She would bring him down to meet me once they could save up enough petrol coupons for his car – 'So I should expect you sometime during 1954 then,' I said. 'Yes,' she said, 'I expect so.' We had wandered back along the West Prom, up the Chine, veering through the tropical garden and onto West Cliff Drive. We arrived back at the Red Villa in need of a strong cup of tea. Mrs Halligan had laid the tea things out in the conservatory. I poured Vivienne a cup. She stood by the doors looking out onto the neglected tennis court, her cup and saucer balanced perfectly in her left hand. Vivienne knew who she was for me, she was the one who treated me exactly as she had always done, without a pause for breath, she resumed being my Vivienne the first minute we saw one another again.

That cold morning in Southampton when I finally arrived home, May 4th 1938, she embraced me in that way only sisters do. I'm embarrassed to say I was so exhausted she had to hold me up a little, but we laughed at this, and this meant we could move forward, through the crowd, into the waiting taxi.

On that drive back to Bournemouth we held hands, she put her head on my shoulder. I didn't say it to Vivienne but I was relieved Mother had not come with her. The taxi wound its way around West Cliff and dropped us at the foot of our drive. The gates to the Red Villa were open and ready to receive us, like they always were when grandmother knew the family were coming from Richmond to visit.

As we walked up the drive the front door opened and Carter appeared. Vivienne had told me that Mother had asked Carter and Lawrence to come, that it would be alright, but when I saw him, standing there in the doorway, I couldn't stop my heart hammering into my spine, I couldn't stop the half-shout caught in my throat. Viv steadied me on my feet. Carter, more emotional than I have ever seen him before or since, squeezed my left shoulder and took my small suitcase. Vivienne and I walked arm in arm through the open door. I heard voices coming from the drawing room, I walked down the familiar hallway, past the photograph of grandmother outside Sydenham's Marine Library, and the photograph of me, all of four years of age, holding Mother's hand on Boscombe pier, the whale skeleton a washed-out spectre behind us.

Lawrence was talking to Mother, she was seated on grandmother's favourite chair, he had his arm across the back of the chair and he was leaning down slightly to speak, a look of great compassion on his face, but she had her head turned slightly away from him, as if the invitation for him and Carter to come was one of the greatest mistakes of her life. Then she looked at me. I will never, in the whole of my life, forget that look. Out from within the cage of her performance came the mother I truly loved, the one I was prepared to fight Beethoven for, the one who used to sing Litanei as I fell into childhood sleep. I saw her but in an instant she was gone, and Mother rose from her seat in perfect time. I walked towards her. She held me by my shoulders, at arms-length, and kissed me. 'So, my dearest,' she said, her voice shaking in its cage, 'you have finally come home.'

I understand now, when I began to fall in love with you, when that long, slow dive commenced. Several weeks after our tennis date, we were leaving Crawford House to have dinner with Carter and Lawrence; we were standing in front of the coat rack in the hallway. I handed you your hat, then put on my own. You studied yourself in the mirror, all the while looking at me as if I was your dresser. Once we were out in the street, you complimented Mother, her aging beauty, her pianist's hands, her impeccable Victorian manners embroidered with fierce pride. You said in other circumstances she would have liked you, even welcomed you, but you and I together, that was too complicated. If you were English, you argued, if you were a nice young man from Oxford who read History and wasn't a socialist, or a communist, you would have been invited back to the next family dinner as my very good friend. But you were a young Berliner, a painter, how could you be anything other than my lover? This was love where love was not supposed to be, she could not embrace you. And as I walked with you, I knew that I couldn't stay, I couldn't live at Crawford House anymore, and all because I told you the time.

There is something about watching a man sleep. You would sleep on your side, knees curled to your chest like a sleeping diver, your left arm flung out into air. You had no sense of the outside world. You smiled slightly, as if you had some secret you weren't about to share with anyone. I would lie awake, looking at you, feeling safe and comfortable, until sleepiness would take me, and I would close my eyes. I fight sleep now. I find myself more rested from naps against the wall than anything else. I wake up seven to eight times a night. Sleep to me is drowning. There is a dark well hidden under my eyelids, and when I close my eyes I fall and I spend the rest of the night fighting to come back up to the light. Viv wants to know what I am planning to do with myself, now I have retired from medicine.

Walking, I tell her. I have a lot of walking to do. I walk out of the town, out along the coast towards Swanage, out to St Alban's Head, edging along the well-worn map of my childhood, not thinking, only breathing, keeping an eye out for the occasional speeding lorry, .the young men on their Triumph motorbikes, the young women on their bicycles. I take a rucksack, and a walking stick of Father's, and I disappear. The light out there is translucent, like the finest seashell.

If I walk far enough out of town, I can find a pub where no one knows me as Dr Carpenter, no one wants to tell me what ails him. I fold myself into a back booth with two pints of watery beer and listen to the talk coming from the bar: National Health Service, Walter Hammond, European Union, Sidney Stanley, Germany, USSR, atomic bombers in Britain. I find myself having no opinions on anything, foreign or domestic. I listen to their arguments, their arm lifter's philosophy, their tones and rhythms, like a mass ob eavesdropper. Courtesy of Viv we have all the back issues of the *Picture Post* at the Red Villa. I flick through them, the war still there in black and white, not quite history yet. I like to read Arthur Ransome's children's books, which were left here in the thirties for Alistair's children. Since coming to stay, Viv has picked up one of my Left Book Club publications, a memoir written by a Viennese doctor who was interned in Birkenau-Auschwitz and then in Dachau. Viv reads this book curled up on the settee, chain-smoking. I have a plan to walk through the New Forest. I have been doing these small, one- to two- to three- to four-mile walks for a while now, mostly in inclement weather, and I think I am almost ready.

John.

June 8th 1969

Dearest Caithleen. This afternoon burning tobacco chased the tips of my fingers. Some ash fell onto the white record and I almost dropped the needle on the vinyl. The notorious dog would not have cared. He ignored me. He watched the rain work its way across the bay. The dog loves you as much as he loves me but I have needed him more. Men and dogs, we can smell each other's loneliness. As you say to me, he is getting older. On that first evening (over four years ago now) when he stood by the fire in the kitchen and pressed his body against my leg, chill had struck him at his heart. I stoked up the fire, made the kitchen red-hot, and drank cold water that I brought in from the laundry sink. Late into the night you sang songs for the dog: 'The Last Rose of Summer', 'Down by the Salley Gardens', 'The Shandon Bells'. And the dog paced the room, he listened to you sing your songs. The sand on his paws fell onto the hard floor like sawdust. He warmed up over some hours, then sometime after midnight, he curled up on the old blankets I had put under the kitchen table for him. And the next morning he took me for my first walk. As we walked, we were a little like the Russian nobleman and his gundog. While we have not shot, fetched, or hunted, our friendship, it is straight from the pages of *A Sportsman's Notebook*. I love him. I am not looking forward to my walk without him through the gates of Heaven or the tunnels of Hell.

This afternoon I started the rock 'n' roll record back at the beginning and I know he was not pleased. I waited for him to speak, to complain to me, but he didn't. He was thinking about walks without me. And so he left after the first few unbearable notes, he took himself for a walk into the village. But he came back during the fourth track. He could not believe I wanted to work with this racket on the radiogram. He stood and whined at the dials, he walked around the stereo to look for a way to tune it into 'The Goon Show'. He barked at me, short sharp barks – he would not work with me like this. I would have to get my own brushes. He left the greenhouse for the rain and the road. I arranged my brushes in good order. I set out enough titanium white. I found two old palette knives at the bottom of a drawer. The painting was shy, quiet, not talking. The music from the radiogram washed over the canvas, and the sounds they picked up dirty flecks of paint, lazy application, underworked lines. And soon the intricate construction of the spine appeared once again. You say that my painting, it reminds you of Anne Madden's *Burren Land*, and yes, I can see this. Her Burren paintings have been burnt into me these last few years. I don't think that I will ever be able to escape them. I take great pleasure from that, from the joy of the new. But I would not have the courage to pour the paint straight onto the canvas like she does. She must have pure, pure faith in her hands, in their dark talent.

On the heels of applause and a rude shout, I heard the weeping guitar (once again). This song is sung by Harrison, the one (I have seen on the television) who always stands in the middle . . . Back. I see you, thirty years ago in London, recovering in hospital. At home, I tore the nursery door off its hinges and wrestled with it down the stairs like it was my drunken uncle, Sergei Dimitrievich. I carried the door outside to the garden shed, and threw it into my nest of torn canvases. I wept and I wept. But a gracious thought came to me from somewhere, an idea. I waded into the canvas with a hammer in my hands. This was when I thought that a clock could be made with the door's lock, a *kulak's* timepiece. Two days later I placed the lock clock on the bedside table. I set it to the correct time. I wound up the mechanism. I watched the hands, willing them to move. That was the night I brought you home from the hospital and I put you to bed. I wanted to say to you, for the past seven nights I have wandered across the Siberian sky. I have drowned in the Dead Sea. I have dreamt of the Arctic Circle. I have slept under your writing desk in my pyjamas. I have asked Shostakovich to write our dead child a concerto. I have manhandled your typewriter and typed a novel of your name. I wanted to say to you, my darling girl, my mother told me when I was a small boy, the night only happens in our dreams, the world is always full of the brightest light, but the minute we close our eyes, darkness pulls us down. But you fell asleep before I could speak. The light on your face flickered and faded as the last small breath of a silent film. I never told you what I did to the nursery door. Only the torn hinges remained.

The white painting took to the rock 'n' roll music. Stopped being so sullen and withdrawn. The paint began to warm up, to turn itself into other shades, other tones so I could work with them and make my mark on the edges of the canvas. Orchestral arrangements blew out of the speakers, then curled and faded as they came. The heavy electric beat returned. Lennon, he loved his girl like a drunken sailor. As you say, my heart is collapsing in a strange, slow way, like old beliefs worn away. This morning, more ordinary poetry. We were curled around one another and the pillows and the sheets. My hands were under your breasts, your back was nestled into my chest, and my heart, it was happy like a drunken bee. We talked quietly, about almost nothing, in that way you like, small talk before your day of writing. I wanted to whisper some Mandelstam into your ear. I wanted to whisper, 'Take from my palms, to soothe your heart/a little honey, a little sun/in obedience to Persephone's bees.' But I couldn't remember the lines without some mistake. When you kissed me, lying in my arms, when you touched my cheek, brushed past it with the tips of your fingers, there was every other time you had performed that gesture, and it was more than memory, more than remembrance, something closer to nature.

For barely shy of forty years I have made love to you. Those months ago now it almost murdered Dr Collins at Clonakilty when I insisted he tell me what it was that I could or could not do in bed with you. We were two old men, Caithleen, between the two of us we had had more sex than any young fella from Cork city. But the sight of a man with no guilt in him, no Catholic shame, terrified an Irishman like the devil himself. And the doctor, he has known you, and your sisters and brothers, since the Celts pole-axed the Normans. But none of that mattered to me, not the doctor's horror at sex, not his relationship with your family. Not the fact he would leave his rooms that day in more need of a whisky than any man in the town. 'To the hairy devil with you, Dr Collins!' I said to him. He sat behind his desk, he hid behind my medical records, my x-rays and my Harley Street notes. He passed paper from his left hand to the right, not able to look me in the eye like a man or answer my plain white questions. Finally, and only because he knew I would never leave his office without an answer, he scribbled down eight instructions, in terse point form, in words so simple a virgin boy of sixteen could have understood what he was saying. I thanked him, and I left him.

This afternoon the paint began to fly from the palette onto the edges of the canvas. Paint curled through the air like white rain. My knife attacked the vertebrae, it cut right through the centre. Underneath McCartney's voice I heard his metronomic boot. His poetry washed out all the unnecessary things and left me alone with my work. As you say, the black coat I was wearing the night we met, it was too beautiful, too elegant. I have never told you, but the coat was Viktor's. It arrived in Billancourt on the back of a stranger. When I arrived in Billancourt I fell in love with a wristwatch. A working-class Parisian's heirloom. This watch, it sat in a shopkeeper's window, so it had weight, meaning, desirability. I had not seen a wristwatch on a civilian since Lenin. So I fell in love with a 1924 Louis Verne, nestled in an original box, with only a slight dent in the stainless-steel casing. It was made for a wrist even thicker than mine, a wrist that could slit the throat of a pig in one graceful arc, or grip the handle of a *porteur* bicycle for miles and miles. But I had no money for this watch. So I wasn't wearing a watch the night I met you in London. And at that time I still dreamt of the large electric clocks bolted into the buildings of Petrograd, demanding our attention, demanding our time.

In my room at the Hotel Caprice, with the blind drawn, I turned Viktor's coat inside out. It hurt to cut out the lining. In the small pockets sewn into the inside of the coat there were three small photographs, family photographs, childhood in Novosibirsk, Mother, Father, small Viktor, small me. And there was a story, a story copied out on thin pieces of paper in writing so small I have always had trouble reading it. I've kept these things in my old suitcase all these years, these things Viktor gave me. No one has ever seen this final story, Viktor's very last story, no one has read it but me. It was because of this story that Viktor was arrested (once again), or because suddenly he was a *kulak*, or (once again) a Trotskyite, or a wrecker and a saboteur, or had foreign connections – such as a brother who had recently received Stalin's permission to leave the Soviet Union for France. Or like millions of others, he was arrested for no reason. My own photographs, my papers, are strewn about the house, the artefacts of a life. But these gifts from Viktor, I have kept to myself. You don't know Viktor, my brother, I have kept him from you, from everyone, here deep in my heart. What should I say about him? What could I begin to tell you now? Well.

Viktor's very first published story made me laugh the night I read it. It made me laugh in a way I imagined opened all the windows above and below us, the Nevsky Prospect tenants leaning out and then suddenly remembering themselves, shutting their windows tightly, smashing their blinds shut in horror at what they had just done, the looking out, the wondering. That night I smiled and laughed in the lamplight (our electricity syphoned, stolen or disconnected). It was a story that Viktor had started to write hours after the October Revolution, when it and he were both young. It was comic, heroic, pro-Soviet and published five times in five different literary journals from 1922-1925. It bought him a new winter coat, three pairs of boots, one or two or three literary subscriptions, and it paid our rent for the whole of 1923. The story was called 'The Black Cat of Petrograd'.

The story began, one winter night at the end of 1912. Nikolai the Fur, official black cat of Alexander Palace, slept in a sable-lined oaken box curled around several Fabergé eggs, dined on duck livers, cream and pheasant, and he was Princess Anastasia's closest familiar. One cold black night in a favourite garden of the Tsarista, he climbed a large oak tree. He was trying to murder three young starlings. As Nikolai leapt from one branch to another, the birds scattered like gunshot. Nikolai's diamond-encrusted leather collar caught on a sharp branch. It threatened to hang him like a common murderer. He was pampered, yes, he was spoilt, but he was still, deep in his heart, a cat. Nikolai twisted and pulled himself out of the collar, popping like a cork out of a champagne bottle. He fell into the air, executed a very decent double somersault and landed on all four paws, shaking his head and unfurling his tail. Slightly irritable, he searched the grounds for Aleksandr Petrovich Okorokov, royal driver and Nikolai the Fur's appointed valet and bodyguard. Nikolai found him, smoking by one of the official cars. Nikolai meowed at A.P. Okorokov for some warm milk and French cognac to recover his nerves. He was greeted, not with the usual histrionic affection Aleksandr gave to him, but with a gruff exclamation and a cold, hard boot to his ribs.

The shock of this sent Nikolai running in a wild panic to the kitchens, where he was always greeted with great love and the finest quality duck livers. But when he got to the kitchens major chef 39 bellowed at him and minor chef 32 threw a bloodied knife at him, narrowly missing the tip of his tail. Minor chef 32 shouted at one of the kitchen boys to fill up a basin of water and throw it on 'the homeless black scoundrel' and as the boy was obeying the order like a military command, Nikolai turned tail. He ran out of the kitchens, out of the palace, through the grounds and dived headlong into the outside world, Tsarskoye Selo, a place he had never seen before. In that village, Nikolai the Fur had his feline eyes opened by the day-to-day fight for home, warmth and bread. Several distinguished Soviet historians note Nikolai's presence in St Petersberg-Petrograd-Leningrad at crucial clandestine meetings, rowdy demonstrations and secret midnight presses. In this way, Nikolai the Fur became Comrade Nikolai. He can be seen in several photographs of Comrade V.I. Lenin, curled into the top right-hand corner of Lenin's writing desk – a thin black question mark, as alert as an assassin's handgun.

I have set down certain sentences from this story verbatim, word for word, communist cadence for communist cadence. Can you almost see this young man, this writer, my brother, whom I have hidden from you all these years? Viktor my brother, he had the soul of a composer, the mind of a member of the intelligentsia, and the cunning of Ostap Bender. His ghost is in the blood that still warms my fingers. This afternoon, I played the first two sides of the white record (again and again), over and over. The notorious dog appeared just as I had cleaned my brushes. He slunk in, he looked for sounds he didn't like, but the radiogram had shut down. Now my white painting looked like a totem, something carved out of chalk, something to ward away evil, not modern at all, not of this century.

You have worked in your study all day, brilliant in your forgetfulness. Caithleen. We have grown old.

As I write this I look at the photograph of Klee in his Weimar studio. The palm of his right hand cradles his head as he studies the camera, his curiosity bleeding through the print. In this photograph Klee is content with small happiness, like a child after a day in the woods, tinkering with the universe. Only eleven years later and he is an enemy of the Third Reich, his Dessau apartment searched, his art classified as degenerate. What would have happened to him had he not gone home to Bern? Another year, perhaps as little as a month, some uniform would have taken a match to his work, splintered the frames, torn the canvas, destroyed him. As you say, Klee's scrying sun allows everything else to live. When I look at *Ad Marginem* for too long, there is a collapse between my eye and the painting, so the world of the painting includes me, but only my shoulders, that can be seen in the bottom left-hand corner of the frame, in the faintest outline of Viktor's black coat, the one brought to me in Paris from Novosibirsk. You are there too, at the top of the painting, but only your shadow as you leave the frame, having stepped gingerly over the long flat length of the red-eyed bird.

Yours, Dmitri.

11 June 1969

Dear Dmitri,

That fat, tattered suitcase you had with you at the Hotel Caprice and then at the Bloomsbury Hotel – that fat, tattered suitcase which has always lived somewhere in our houses, the kitchen, the pantry, the laundry, under the stairs – now I know it is full of Viktor's handwriting! You have barely mentioned your brother all these years, and I have always understood. He has been your secret. Thank you for opening the suitcase. Thank you for speaking of him to me. I have always thought you should be the one telling stories, that it was a more natural thing for you, and perhaps Viktor has something to do with this, with your ease not only with words but with the horrible fact that writing is like any other work. When I dig in for years and even away from the typewriter can't hear anything else; you have always known exactly what to do with me. I want to thank you for being in the room with me when I was learning to be a writer. I remember how, years ago in London, you would sit near me surrounded by thirty or forty books of poetry, English, Irish, Russian (official), Russian (unofficial), a little French, a little German. You would read a poem or so from each of them, picking them up and putting them down like women's magazines. I can see you now! You never disturbed me, you simply smoked and read while I worked and swore. When I became too disturbed you would stand by the desk, could you have this dance? Then we would take a fanciful turn around the room, dodging the book stacks. Sometimes we would end up in the bedroom. Sometimes I would end up back at the typewriter. These are like lantern-slides that will stay alight in my mind. Somehow, in between the reading and the dancing and the lovemaking, a novel was completed. You knew what I didn't – that my writing had not hit its target yet, but that I had to keep drawing the bow.

At the London press conference, all those years ago, I remember, when the journalists asked you about your life in London, your upcoming, first exhibition at Wertheim Gallery, how polite you were: you answered all their questions thoughtfully and carefully; but you also had a decade of other things to say and they came out of your mouth like perfect circles of barbed wire, sharp, hot and direct. That was what I saw the first time I ever saw you.

I watched James, writing faster than any man there, thinking faster than any man there, knowing he'd get more from you in the bar later, that he wouldn't waste his breath with tepid questions, what he wanted was a good look at you, an observation of your character.

I never told you why I was in London that night. Once you and I saw one another we ran fast into courtship, into simply being together.

It was a standard journalist joke that James had brought his *Cork Examiner* harem along for the trip, that he couldn't stand to be in England without the company of good Irish women and sisters to boot. I was there because I could be chaperoned by Claire who was there because she was James's wife. She was the perfect alibi for my escape from my parents and from Cork; I was the perfect alibi for her, the younger sister to be kept on the straight and narrow. At that point no one knew I wasn't planning to return to Cork. It had come to be expected that I would be the one to stay. That until I married, I would work at the Dunbar Street creamery, oversee the girls there. By that point all of my brothers had gone, Patrick, Francis, Ronan, Connor. They wanted nothing to do with butter, nothing to do with tea. Claire and I were made to promise by our parents that we would share a room while in London. It was too dangerous, a young girl in a strange city, I could not be alone.

James would amble down the corridor of the hotel at one o'clock in the morning and, without breaking stride, slide a blank white piece of paper under our door, then walk on past our room along the hall and around the corner to the Gents'. I would come out of our room, dressed as if I was coming back from a late theatre engagement, my nightie curled up in my handbag along with a second copy of James's room key. I spent four hours a night in his dishevelled bed, fag ends and half-drunk beer bottles littered around, sleeping awake waiting for the white paper signal I could go back to our room. Then I would walk back, at five in the morning (!) looking like a lady of the night, not a lady of the theatre any more. And they really fell in love then, James and Claire, you could see it in their bodies, when they walked together, arm in arm like the sweethearts they were.

Dmitri. I remember, after we had that first drink together, the next day you took me to Soho, and you bought newspapers and tobacco. I can still see the details of that day. You only bought the newspapers because it looked like it would rain and you had left your umbrella back at the hotel. The tobacco was for me. Somehow you could tell I was a secret smoker. It surprised me when you invited the tobacconist to the opening of your exhibition. You told him there was nothing radical to see, but perhaps he was curious anyway. As we left, you opened the door out of the little tobacconist's, raised the papers in a mock salute and we were gone. Later, that shopkeeper did come to see your paintings. He said to me they were like walking through a summer storm. And do you remember that at the exhibition opening you drank far too much? By the end of the evening, James was holding you up by your cuff links. Perhaps you don't remember.

I remember the first time we made love; just before, you took off your shirt and I saw your scars for the first time, running the length of your back like fits of rope, and I burst into tears. We had married that morning, and I was feeling that strange, unfamiliar truth and I sobbed like I had been there when this terrible thing had happened to you, as if I had watched it happen and I was powerless to do anything for you, anything at all. You whispered things to me, I don't remember exactly what, but you held me and you whispered, telling me they didn't matter, what had happened didn't matter, there was no pain there for you now, you were alright. You kissed my eyelids, my forehead, you wouldn't touch me until I was completely calm, and completely quiet. And I loved you more for that, there, in that moment before you and I were together for the first time.

Now, back here in the present, you write to me about ordinary things. Ordinary poetry. That is where the true art exists. Take this morning, my love. This morning, I took my daily bath in breaking light, my body old and adrift in the smoky water. I had sweet, stewed tea, and the *Cork Examiner,* which hovered above the waterline. I find myself drawn to reading about the North, the Civil Rights Marches, the riots. Granny used to talk of some distant cousins in Enniskillen, but I could walk by them in the street now and not know them at all. Seated in our old collapsed chair, you sipped weak coffee and examined the line of my neck. I'd tied my hair back, a single strand curled around my ear like a silver treble clef. You went downstairs to pour me a second cup of Barry's tea. When you came back up, I had folded up the paper as carefully as origami. We exchanged one for the other, paper for chipped china cup. I took a long drink from this second cup of tea. I swung the cup around with a flick of my fingers. Quietly, I told you to undress. You took off your shirt and hung it on the back of the old chair, your scars still alive and running across your back. You undid your trousers, stepped out of them, folded them up and placed them neatly on the chair. I handed you my tea cup and you put it under the chair beside your coffee glass. I stood up carefully and stepped out of the bath. We kissed. Beads of water collapsed on my skin. You dried me, then slid your hands from my shoulders to the lock of my hips. I placed my arms around your neck, and you cradled my backside. We went into the bedroom. Words caught in my throat. I kissed you behind your left ear then held your face in my hands. I looked into your burnt eyes. You whispered something. I moved to rest my back against the pillows. I laid my left hand on my knee, palm open, fingers outstretched. You put your hands on the inside of my thighs. You bowed down and ran your tongue over my clitoris. Beads of light rose and broke in my mind's eye. Since we have come back to live full time in the south-west, these past five years, I have dreamt of a little girl, blond and a bit tall for her age, carrying a long black cat over her shoulder like an afterthought, singing not to herself but to God, loud, so very loud, while she walks through the long summer grass near the woodlands. I dream of this little girl who never tells me her name, who never comes into Granny's house, but who takes strong cups of Barry's tea from me on the doorstep like a tradesman, talking about the soft weather, and the price of milk. She sits in the greenhouse though, on one of the old tea crates, her long black cat stretched across her lap, his beautifully shaped paws flicking out at invisible, dreamt-up mice. She sits and she makes up songs, strange rambling numbers about trips in the village lifeboat, and the biggest bowl of ice-cream in County Cork.

She sits and waits for you but you never arrive. And she never seems to care, though I know she really does, and she knows too, but we never speak of it, she and I; only of the weather, and the price of milk. I wake myself up crying, and never tell you why. I can't speak of her now, I couldn't speak of her then. We loved her so much, you and I, though we only had her for such a small time, that miracle growing inside me, that beautiful, beautiful girl. In those first months of pregnancy I spent hours trying on names like fancy hats: Katherine, Carmel, Terese, Mary, Claire, Margaret. I never asked you for your thoughts, I was fierce in my wanting to name her myself, to come to you with the perfect name, the only name so you couldn't argue with me –

I remember, you remember, we could never forget that morning, September 3rd '39, that morning in the London house, how the words falling out of the radio made horrible sense. Another war was coming. The second shot. You offered me your hand. I took it and leant into you as I stood up, almost losing my balance. You kissed me. The Virginia roses covering my old dress seemed to smell of rain and perfume. And when, a week or so later, my world collapsed, when I fell down hard and broke everything, my bones, my heart, my skull, Claire ran all the way from Cork to London. And you, my darling boy, you never seemed to sleep. You never seemed to move from that chair beside my hospital bed. When I was well enough, it was agreed we would go home to Cork, to live with James and Claire in the city, it was all agreed upon, at least until this new war was over.

I made a telephone call to Claire from Fiona's this morning. She is already organising the Nieces and the children, even though it's a few weeks before they come and stay. On the telephone this morning, Claire, because she is Claire, asked about your health, and the world dissolved, spiralled away. Claire nudged me. I said we couldn't know if anything we did for you made a difference at all. Claire said to me, did I remember the time that she and I, all of eight and six years, spent a Saturday afternoon dropping pieces of bread into O'Driscoll's well. We could hear the coo of an injured dove trapped on a ledge, but he was wrapped in darkness. We had no idea if any of the bread we dropped would reach him, but we felt we had to help. Granny punished us for wasting four whole slices on a half-dead bird, and for spoiling O'Driscoll's water with specks of bread. Claire was indignant at her punishment, and exploded with the wrath of a wronged woman – while I, Claire reminded me now, had pondered the moral failings that had led me to the decision to try and help a feeble bird that the Lord our God had, in His wisdom, marked for death. I laughed. She said we should try and find any family you might still have, we should buy a God-fearing Irish homing pigeon, tie a note to his leg and send him off to Petrograd with the protection of Saint Finbarr.

She said that the girls had had a laugh about your sudden interest in electric guitars. They wondered if they should bring their dear old uncle some more rock 'n' roll records. I said I didn't know. You hated Bing Crosby, Frank Sinatra and Elvis when they came along. But you listened to these white songs as if they were Bach cantatas. I said to Claire that I suspected the notorious dog of plotting against the band, waiting for the moment he could put some carefully chosen teeth marks into their evil circles of plastic. She laughed, and said the girls and their broods were looking forward to seeing you, to being with us all at Granny's, something they hadn't done for years. They loved us, Claire said, like the whole sky itself. It was good to hear. I think we have done the right thing, my dear, coming home for good. I am happy we are here now and nowhere else. But truth be told, my dearest boy, I am tired tonight. The long day has brought me nothing but memories.

Caithleen.

9/10/2011

Hey Lou,

It's late. The easterly is rolling over the back garden, waltzing with the Chinese elm, telling late night stories to whomever will listen. Bonnie and Clyde are still up and prowling about. I was washing the dishes in the kitchen and I saw the two of them out the window. Along they came, tiptoeing across the fence like Siamese acrobats, on their way to trouble. We're lucky they get on with Crow Bait, considering how much time they spend in our garden. On cool days I still find the three of them in their favourite daytime place, curled up on the boxes in the shed, fast asleep. And of course Crow Bait misses you. Every morning without fail he comes into the bedroom, head-butts me awake, meowing, and begins his search for you – under the covers, under the bed, even in the wardrobe. After all these years he still doesn't understand where you go and why you go, he has never got used to it. When his search is over, when he can't find you, he lets out one mighty meow of protest and leaves in a huff. I'm okay but he loves you the best, ever since he set eyes on you. We've always known this. You, then Patrick, then Pete, then Nate, then me, that's always been his order of affection. It's late, Lou. I miss you. There is no remedy for the late night alone. I don't know. Those bloody cranes all over the city are getting to me again. I know it's not new, in fact as long as I can remember there has been a crane or two in the city skyline, even back in the 1970s, remember, when the tallest building in Perth was the AMP building, back in the day when all us Perth kids had to look forward to each year was Telethon, the Choc Milk Regatta and the Christmas Pageant. But those 1970s cranes, there were maybe one or two then, now it's cranes everywhere, in every viewpoint. I defy anyone to take a picture of the city without a fucking crane in it. Those mechanical birds oversee the frantic building going on, in the streets below and in the sky above, waiting to catch some poor bastard if he makes the wrong two-step on the skeleton of a fiftieth floor. But Lou, no one has told the property developers that the City of Perth is too small for all of this frantic big city beeswax. It's got worse even since you left this time. It's now impossible to walk in the city, to stroll. Footpaths are blocked, whole streets are cordoned off, trucks too wide and too long rumble past penned mobs of pedestrians, trucks carrying girders, concrete blocks, impossibly long steel pipes. People are pissed off, frustrated, searching like a football crowd for the easiest way out, for the easiest way to get where they want to go. They jostle and dodge, agitated by the no-access, the stop-and-turn-around, the walk-on-the-other-side. We're not used to it, this sustained largesse, but believe it or not, there is a 21st century metropolis blooming right in front of us. All the new shiny things of the city are disturbing me.

This morning I sat in the bookshop under muggy yellow light cleaning books from a deceased estate in Tyrell Street. Most of them had been originally purchased decades ago at Alberts, and probably had never been out of Nedlands. Crow Bait prowled around the books, chatting and purring, chasing the odd silverfish too quick for his old cat body. The lack of spring rain brought out the usual banter from the customers – well what will happen to the wheat belt, it should be raining I just pegged the washing out, we need at least a week of good rain to add something to the dams. I had to go around the shop with the washing basket – some UWA girls nattering on their smartphones. They looked at me like I had asked them to sever their right arms from their shoulders, but being polite, well-bred young ladies they surrendered their phones. It made them twitch, and clutch each other for support, but they got through it. Nate was right when he told me no one under forty would take my sign seriously.

I don't know. I was not exactly lost before I met you but I wasn't exactly found either. I've made a living out of the only thing I could do well, reading, and I was content curled up in my tiny bookshop with the Whitlock boys for love and company. I think that Dad would have been much happier if I had become an accountant like him, or an optometrist, 'a good career for girls', he once said to me. But if I was never going to pursue a proper career, at least I had his single-bloody-mindedness. When I met you, and I was working down at Serendipities in West Leederville, I think I was already plotting and scheming to get my own shop. And when Trinity Arcade happened, Dad was so proud. He loved coming down the first of every month to do the books with me. You remember, we did them the old-fashioned way, no software, all ledgers. Sometimes I go back over those old ledgers now just to see his handwriting, his little queries in the margins like tiny fatherly advice. He loved you. I know he never said it but you have to believe me when I say it's true. He knew you would bring me out of myself, show me the world, you know? He was happiest when I'd tell him we were off on holiday again, he wanted me to leave Perth again and again, so I could appreciate what I had, too, so I would not be complacent and take it for granted. Or worse, begin to believe what those eastern states wowsers said about us. He loved Melbourne, because it was the home of real football, and the home of his beloved Carlton Football Club. He loved going to Young & Jackson's for a beer, he'd take in a show at the Forum Theatre, and he'd catch up with old friends in Moonee Ponds. But he would always ring me, from the hotel or the pub, to tell me he missed the light. He wasn't sentimental, Dad, not remotely, but the West had him by the scruff of the neck, it was home to him. And he admired you, for being who you were, fix-it woman to the rich and famous, but happiest when you were on Leighton Beach, watching the country's luckiest dogs run amok in the sand and the sea. He really did.

Pete came into the bookshop in the early afternoon. Recently he has taken to calling it the Tardis, adding to his standard joke that 'the joint is not big enough to swing Crow Bait in'. He kissed me on the cheek, then handed me a cup of Lady Grey and a lamington from the Forum Coffee Shop. I showed him the antique postcard Nate had sent me, entitled *New York View from Brooklyn.* The postcard showed the Manhattan skyline, Brooklyn Bridge, tug boats on the Hudson. In 1912 it would have cost Nate one cent for domestic postage, or two cents for foreign postage. Pete sat on the stepladder and we chatted a bit. Nate had found some Park Slope digs; he was happy with the pianist the show had found for him; but he'd gotten so nervous about his German he'd started taking cheap lessons from a German expat holed up in some boarding house in Brooklyn. While we chatted, books landed on the counter like legs of lamb. Charmaine Clift, Eleanor Dark, Doris Lessing, Edna O'Brien, Iris Murdoch. I wrapped them in plain brown paper and sent them out into the world with their new readers. I don't know how or even why but they're still coming, the readers. As I've said to you before over a cup of tea, maybe it's Trinity Arcade that draws them first, its art deco beauty; and being people attracted to such things, they automatically wander into the bookshop. I've never told you this but I often fantasise about the man who buys some Wembley Ware at Trinity Antiques, is fitted for a Paul Smith suit at Parker's, then comes into the bookshop and purchases my first edition *Ulysses*. The thought of his arrival keeps me going, some weeks. But until he arrives I must be content with my ramshackle collection of customers. At one point when the shop was empty, Pete looked about, at the shelves bursting with books, piles of books on the floor, on the desk, behind the doors and he said to me, 'All these bloody books, Grace, it's a bit like collecting death, isn't it?' I don't know. It seemed true, when he said it, when it was only him and me and Crow Bait, who was rolling on the desk, batting my arm. I looked at Pete, the one Whitlock who never read, who as a kid was too busy kicking, throwing, or chasing a ball, and I thought, for you Pete, yes, it's true, you have no use for the stories of other people. But for me, they are everything I've known, everything I ever had, everything came from them. And I said to him, 'Only if the books are never read.' Pete laughed and got up off the stepladder. He had to go back down Stirling Highway to the Black Swan. He said if he left the young blokes in charge for too long they started getting ideas about how to brew the beer. He keeps telling them they haven't been drinking long enough yet to appreciate the subtleties. I wonder how my brother is, you know? He keeps himself to himself, works hard, loves his son, but we don't talk like he and Patrick did. Brothers I suppose, but he knows and I know that every time we see one another, we still expect Patrick to burst into the room from somewhere and take over the conversation, the afternoon and the night. And when that doesn't happen, we both feel a little bit older. I decided not to tell Pete about the dream I had about Nate. It was a few nights ago now. I was having a restless time anyway as Crow Bait was in and out, his dodgy bladder giving him all the wrong signals. In my dream the world was shot in sepia, and Nate was staying at a grand Italian villa. Like Orsino in *Twelfth Night*, Nate had injured his arm, it was in a sling. He was sitting at a wrought-iron table in one of the gardens with another young man who was also injured, with a badly sprained ankle and two cracked ribs. Looking out from the main terrace at the two young men was the owner of the villa, himself a Count, a kind, intelligent man of impeccable manners and taste. This man was smoking and watching the two young men play a board game. This board game involved the use of dice and of cards. The name of this game was printed on the box: Auto-de-Fé. The font of Auto-de-Fé was quite beautiful. As the Nate in the dream is safe, his boyfriend safe, and obviously both well cared for, the dream doesn't worry me too much, except perhaps for the board game. But I think it is like this. Nate is not a young gay man who will ever play it straight. He tried, tried so hard when he was fifteen, sixteen, but it just wasn't him. He's not an out-there queen, but you'd be hard pressed not to spot him. Now he is not in Perth, I find that difficult not to be frightened about. It only takes thirty seconds for something to happen. Yes, New York is crawling with queers, thousands of us, but the homophobia remains, and it's been acting up of late, if it ever went away at all (do you know about the Yankee fans' homophobic version of YMCA?). I'm not picking on New York, that's just where Nate happens to be at the moment, you know? And Nate, he's cocky like his uncle, with an accent like a boundary rider, as subtle as a bloody chainsaw. I sometimes wish he were an accountant like his grandfather. That he was the kind of guy who would settle down with some perfectly nice public servant called Andrew, be mortgaged to the hilt in Bayswater, and who would, on public holiday weekends, take his boyfriend and their two border collies (Armistead and Maupin) away to an eco-retreat in Margaret River. I sometimes wish he wasn't so Nate, so bloody noticeable, so bloody available, collecting boyfriends like swap cards. When he was very little, before you and me, he used to call me Aunty Mum. He grew out of it by the time he was six years old but I don't think I have. I suppose I have to look to Pete on how to play this. He's not worried, because he made Nate do all the right things (register his trip, triple copy his documents) and because knowing my brother, he has an emergency plan to go to New York in case Nate needs him. So Pete laughs, and I worry, these are the gender roles neatly sliced, as Aunty Mum I can't get away from them.

You and I . . . we've had our share of public

incidents over the years, from mumbled insults to out-and-out confrontations, but the older we get, the more we pass for straight women, which disturbs me on one level and relieves me on another. We've talked about this many times. Now we are no longer young enough to want our heads shaved or to own twelve-hole Doc Martins, we are constantly mistaken for sisters, or cousins or best friends. The revelation is treated as a gentle in-joke, but is that progress? I'm not so sure. I'm still not comfortable holding hands in public, let alone kissing. You have a different opinion but you've never pushed the issue. So we've developed a complicated and rather ornate set of hand movements designed to touch the lower back, the neck, the shoulder, the hip; a form of non-sexual public intimacy which is both ambiguous and absolutely definite. As if the public performance is the last taboo, and still the most dangerous thing to do. Do you remember our first proper date, the first one after our meeting at Nate's birthday party – when we met at the West Australian Art Gallery? An exhibition of Irish Modernist Painters . . . I remember that the one painting which had everyone talking, in fact the only painting that I can still remember after all these years, was that long white painting which was hanging in the main space. It looked like they had to rearrange a few walls to get it in there. Some people hated it, or thought it was a joke, but you and I, we spent a good half an hour in front of it. And I recall that we did manage some conversation about the painting, some good runs at it, like a rusty vaudeville act thrown on a stage, trying to hold it together for the folks. Weirdly, I remember your voice, how hard I listened to your voice, for what I don't know, some kind of affirmation of your kindness, your goodness, your worth. There was attraction, of course attraction, but not that dramatic, smack-me-down type. I was relieved – that kind of attraction had always got me into trouble before, like kidding yourself you can handle a fast car. We were curious about one another, and that was enough to make us want to see each other again, that and a smouldering suspicion that if I kissed you the world might illuminate. Grace.

18th October 2011

Oh Grace. Grace, Grace, Grace. It's a dead blue late night here, too cold even for the Berliners. The rain goes on and on. I am in the hotel bar with Stow. We have taken over the place so we can get through another mega round of interviews. Stow hates being locked in his hotel room with a circus of journos, he can't stand it so we do it like this every now and then. It's a bloody headache for us and for hotel management, but no one is going to tell him it can't be done. The German bodyguards are with us while the Australians are guarding all entrances and exits. A scrum of photographers are camping outside (they'll stay there unless they want to be bundled up in a headlock and thrown back into the night). Stow scrolls through his emails while he tells a *Vanity Fair* journalist about his childhood watching wild clouds burst over Calgardup Bay. Since waving journalists in and out of the bar is not a difficult task I've got the assistants doing it. I'm going to sit on the sidelines for a little while and write this letter to you. God knows I don't need to hear Stow being interviewed thirty times; and he's so Zen I won't have to worry about him saying something stupid. So I'm drinking whisky and listening to 'Time' (*The Revelator*). Gillian Welch's call and response with Dave Rawlings has such complications, you have to listen with the whole weight of your heart; there's no other way than at the slow speed of a needle on a record. Our first date, really? How do you remember the sound of my voice then? You must have been looking for signs and wonders. I do remember noticing your hands, watching you pour that cup of peppermint tea we had at The Moon, not really listening to what you were talking about, something about your brothers, I think. And it took half-a-dozen dates before our first kiss (what were we doing, following some Victorian handbook on the art of female friendship?). And you damn well know how much I hate not being able to kiss you in public. I would if you would let me, I would hold your hand as well, but I suppose I understand why you won't. Your Nate dream is like a tab of ecstasy designed by Italo Calvino. Good God, Grace, please try to not worry so much about him! All those years on the footy field taught him how to handle himself. He'll be alright. Good on him for sending you postcards. I found him some Paul O'Montis on vinyl yesterday. Nate keeps calling me to practise his German (I don't know why when mine is passable at best). What a strange thing for Pete to say – collecting books, collecting death. When I come into your bookshop (and dutifully hand over my BlackBerry like a gunslinger at a church) I feel free, and curious. I don't know what I am going to find in all those books. I wonder which is the right way to fix this, to bring us back together again. We're like a broken but beautiful watch. I love your letters, the way they draw me back to you, the way they draw me back home again. I'd forgotten how much I love your simplicity; the way you love the people and things you love, and how you are satisfied with that. You know me, Grace. I am restless, irritated, frustrated, never satisfied with anything I do. There always has to be more, there always has to be the next thing. I push through the world, charge through it and don't even breathe. It doesn't occur to me to stop, it doesn't occur to me to take stock. I don't know how to stay in one place. I think this is why I like such old-fashioned music, its time is slow and steady and of one place within one voice. It asks you to sit and to stay and to listen and not to do too much or you'll ruin the prayer of it, you'll miss the point of it all. So I'm trying to be in one place, if only for the next small while. My BlackBerry is turned off. I am not planning anything. There is only the whisky and the water and the music. These words on the page, the constant coming in and going away of journalists, the steady presence of Stow in the bar, the whole show orbiting around him, but never touching him, never even coming close. And I can breathe. You matter to me. You matter to my life in ways I can't comprehend. I only know how much you mean when I am off balance, when I am threatened with tipping over some invisible edge. I'd like to understand that I love you when I feel steady and alright (that would be good, that would work). Gillian is singing about dreaming a highway back to you. I want to do that, I wish I could do that. I have to do that now. I have to turn around and start walking back towards you but it's become a long way. I've been gone for years and years. But that is no revelation. Loneliness. Its long white feathers drop and gather around my feet, they blow out of the bar, under the hotel doors and out into the street, into the rain. I want you here and I can't make it happen. I want to kiss you in that way we used to all those years ago. I want to sleep with you. Rest my soul. Gillian is singing,

You be Emmylou and I'll be Gram,
I sent a letter, don't know who I am.

Louise.

June 4th–6th '48

Dearest David,

My war is now a magic lantern of the mind. Circular slides set in wooden frames. Home from sixteen hours at Hahnemann House, curled into a corner of the settee, wrapped in an old olive-green cardigan of my father's, drinking his whisky, pouring pure light into my famished body. Standing at the bar of the Metropole Hotel with a Canadian airman, both of us thoroughly drunk, talking Canadian cricket, the legendary Jack Laing. Back at Hahnemann House, scrubbing after surgery, soaping my hands, forearms and elbows, warm water curling over the white basin, the thin red soup going down the drain, barley sugar under my tongue. The dull white of an air battle peeling back the Bournemouth night, enemy aircraft turning and shifting with anaesthetic slowness. It's been four years since

D-Day, three since VE Day, and Mrs Halligan still won't leave me to fend for myself, there is too much between us now. We have never talked about you, but these things have a way of seeping through the furniture. To her, you are my Viennese friend.

Viv still interrogates Mrs Halligan about my well-being, my drinking and anything else she can think of; Mrs Halligan stands firm, and only tells her what is necessary, what I've been eating, if I've been resting, how many sleeping pills I've taken. She has never mentioned other, stranger things to Viv. We are bound together, Mrs Halligan and I, by small secrets. I am grateful for her kindness. Sometimes I think that is all that keeps me in Bournemouth. But there is nowhere else for me to go. Vienna has been fractured. I remember the night Hitler arrived at the Imperial Hotel, March 11th '38. Schuschnigg made his announcement on the radio, 'I yield to force . . . God protect Austria!' and a huge crowd swarmed through the Ringstrasse, carrying swastika flags and singing the 'Horst Wessel Lied'. You burnt illegal political papers over the toilet and flushed the remnants away. We delivered into safe hands those two false Czech passports we were holding on to for Gregory. We waited in our apartment all the next day.

Our first time in bed together, our first day in Carter and Lawrence's convenient Chelsea flat, I told you that I wasn't much of a swimmer as a boy (not like you and your years of schoolboy competitions) but I was an excellent diver. My father had taught me during a chilly Bournemouth summer when I was ten years old. He spent hours with me, hours over days and days and when I was finally ready, when it came to me standing on the springboard at the end of the pier, I believed my life was about to change forever. It was not the only time I remember being close to him, not the only time I remember him being proud of me. But nothing after that, not the tennis, not the school grades, seemed to give him as much pleasure as my first real dive. It was a perfect moment for both of us, an arc of happiness not to be repeated.

You and your father never had even a minute of closeness. First the art, then the boys separated you forever. You were unknown to him, as foreign as China. Your mother did not treat you any better or any worse for being a queer. She didn't reject or protect you, but overnight the relationship between you and your mother changed forever. How you came to be in bed with me that day is astounding to me.

You said men before me were fun, but they were not curious about you, they only wanted you. But that first time I looked at you, you thought I was going to bring out my doctor's pad and begin taking notes. I studied you. And you found that attractive. I told you sex for me had been like a game of tennis. I would choose a partner for his potential to match me, then I would invite him to play. I had deliberately avoided any emotional entanglements because I told myself that my work came first, and anyway love was a sentimental thing, something women got themselves trapped by, it wasn't for me. Life was too serious for love. I never waited to get to know a man before I had him. I didn't want to know him, I had no intentions of knowing him, and once I had slept with him, I never saw him again. But I confessed to you that there was one man before who had raised my interest.

I can still remember his cologne and the way he looked out of a train window, as if the view was going to be the most important one of his life. He was unusual in that he didn't read a newspaper on the train, he didn't keep himself to himself, he dared to look around at the people, at the view and then back to the people again. He never tried to strike up a conversation with strangers, that would have been quite inappropriate, but he noticed people, and they noticed him noticing them. It struck me that he was happy, happy to be sitting in that train carriage. It was understood, between him and I, that he was 'so', and so was I. I never pursued him because I didn't want to be disappointed. I doubted

I could carry it off, this interest beyond sex. But that was before I met you. That was why I invited you for tennis. You were the second man to raise my interest, and the only man I made aware of the fact.

I remember on that first day in bed with you I ate an apple, a warm golden apple the colour of nectar, and I looked up at the ceiling. I would do this hundreds of times over the years, this was a ritual, a daily habit of mine. I told you this was how I gave up smoking. I still carried my silver cigarette case stacked with Players but I no longer smoked them. Instead I ate an apple a day, chewing slowly and thinking. You asked me for one of my cigarettes and I obliged you. You blew smoke at the ceiling while I worked my way around my apple in an anti-clockwise direction. You pretended to be as deep in thought as I obviously was but really you were thinking about how long it would be before you got to kiss me again. I told you that this was the first time I had stayed in bed with a man after sex. If I were to be honest, I said, most of the sex did not happen in a bedroom. University rooms, hotels, Brighton dunes, a car in a country lane. This was new for me, this desire to be with someone like this. You asked me why and I asked what did you mean. You said why me. I'd finished my apple by then. I took what was left of the cigarette out of your hand and stubbed it. Then I kissed you, very softly, almost delicately. I said that the answer to that question was the reason I was here, and no doubt I would stay here even when I had the answer. And I kissed you again. On that first afternoon, our first afternoon together, we were only at the beginning, at the beginning of everything, when we hadn't reached love but the ghost of it was there with us in the room, the third, uninvited guest.

John.

June 9th '48

Dearest David,

My first three letters to you are burning a small, surgical hole in the inside pocket of my suit jacket which is hanging in my wardrobe. George C. has come to mind. George C. was a gentleman of the road who would turn up at Barts three or four times a year. George had no fixed address, he would walk the length and breadth of Kent looking for his wedding ring. George had sold his wedding ring to a bloke in a Kentish pub one bloody wet, dark, wailing drunken night and he couldn't remember where, only that the place smelt of fish and behind the bar there was a painting of a small white cat in a blue basket. This particular time that he came to see me at the hospital he was in a much worse state than usual – I'd only patched him up before – but this time his temperature was terribly high. I snuck him down to an out-of-the-way ward and sweet-talked the Sister to take him, telling her he was an old Army friend of my father, I would pay his bills and would she make an exception to the rules just this once. Not believing my story for a second she ordered one of the nurses to give George a sponge bath and to dress him in a clean pair of hospital pyjamas. When I returned George was propped up in his bed, clutching a brown duffle bag. He wanted to know where his clothes had got to then and I told him that an orderly had whisked them away to be cleaned and pressed, yes even his coat and hat. He smiled at the thought.

I told him I was going to examine him properly now and he said well if I had to, I was the doctor and I knew best. But he wouldn't let go of the duffle bag. I assumed it contained all his possessions in the world. I asked him if he would tell me what was in the duffle bag. 'Well,' said George, 'I wouldn't have thought there was much you hadn't seen, Doctor Carpenter, but if you like.' He told me to hold out my hands. I did. He opened the duffle bag, and very carefully brought out a bottle of Indian ink, which he placed in my left hand. It was almost brand new. Then he brought out a Watermark fountain pen and placed that in my right hand. It was a beautiful pen, turn of the century, and was engraved with George's full name, including the middle initial. Then George produced from the bag a letter in a stained and torn envelope, and several sheets of almost clean writing paper, which he placed on the bed beside him. He peered into the bag and declared there was nothing else of interest to a doctor such as myself. I placed the inkbottle and the pen on his night table and thanked him for satisfying my curiosity. He asked me if I didn't want to know who the letter was from, then? I said to him that I thought it would be a letter from his wife and he looked at me as if I'd guessed his birthday and said yes, it was, how did I know that? She was dead, no doubt about it, his lovely wife, but he still liked to write to her, tell her all the things he saw on his travels, the strangers he met that became friends, like my good self. I thanked George for the compliment. He grunted and moaned and groaned while I held my stethoscope to his chest and cupped his back. What I heard in his lungs was very bad news. It wouldn't be long before we would be at the crisis point of his pneumonia. I said that I wouldn't muck him about, we'd known each other too long for that. George held up his hand as if he were stopping a car in the street and he said – 'It's alright, Dr Carpenter, there's those who'd say I'm only taking up room in this world meant for others, and if the time's come for me to be put out to be collected, well, at least that'll stop them complaining.' I asked George if there was anyone I could contact for him, to tell them he was in hospital, and he said no, not unless I knew the bloke who'd bought his wedding ring from him in '26. I collected up George's letter and his writing paper and placed them under his ink-bottle. He reached over and placed the duffle bag with the rest of his things under his bed. 'Can't be too careful,' he said. As I was writing up his chart I asked him what he did with the letters he wrote to his wife. He said he sent them, sometimes, to their old address at Folkestone, or to his wife's sister at Maidstone, sometimes he left them in trees if he was camping in the North Downs, sometimes he'd run them in a stream, or a brook. There's always a place for them, he said, always a home. I nodded, and wished him goodnight.

When George died the Sister gave me the duffle bag containing his belongings. I gave his three shillings, two pence to the hospital fund. I turned out his half-bottle of Oldfield's single malt whisky. I had the pen appraised and it was a limited edition Watermark produced in 1910, the last year of King Edward's reign. You couldn't buy these pens, they were given by Queen Alexandra to some of her Buckingham Palace staff. I sent the pen, the letter and the rest of George's things to the address on the back of his wife's letter, her sister's in Maidstone. In the weeks before his death, George had written two letters to his wife so I posted them for him, one in the early morning in an oak tree in a quiet corner of Hyde Park, the other at twilight out of the window of my train. I haven't posted the letters I have recently written to you, but I have wanted to. George and I have more in common these days than we did back then.

I visited Sam Vickers. Are you surprised? There isn't much I ever did that surprised you. I was as easily read by you as that copy of 'Sonette an Orpheus' you carried everywhere. Vickers and I were up at St George's together in the twenties. Except for Carter and Lawrence, he is the only old friend who knows about you. Before I went to see him I told Vickers on the telephone that Viv had been very keen for me to see him in a professional capacity, but I wasn't the least bit interested. I was, however, prepared to come and chat about cricket, Wimbledon, the Olympics, if he had a gap in his schedule. Vickers laughed and agreed on one condition. He wanted to borrow one of your paintings for his rooms. I told Vickers I couldn't simply tuck one of your paintings under my arm like a church fete watercolour. He said he understood. He would send men to Bournemouth to pick up a painting of my choice. I agreed to his price and so sealed the deal. In his Harley Street rooms he was as welcoming as the parish priest. He sat me down in one of his far too comfortable chairs. He offered me tea. He smiled, the calm genuine smile of a confident man voyaging out. We hadn't seen one another for over a year, but there was Vickers all over again, his murky river green eyes, his scruffy blond hair sticking up like an exclamation mark, his little black notebook. We were close, once, a thousand years ago now. He smoked cigars. They helped him think, he said, and without them he chewed his nails down to the quick. There is something instantly calming about an analyst with a compulsion.

As we chatted and swapped war experiences, he sat on the bow of his desk like a disobedient schoolboy and doodled furiously into a black notebook, only stopping to turn and tap the ash from his cigar into an ashtray. As I left Vickers' rooms that day, accompanied by his strong handshake, I thought of my father shaking my hand at Bournemouth station, the morning he saw me off to St George's. I was, in that moment, a young man with promise and skill, as blessed as I was the day I took my first dive. I was still his. On the train home from Vickers' to Bournemouth, I remembered that unusually warm spring afternoon when I surprised you by being home early. I was out of breath, I had run home, clutching a book for you I had wrapped clumsily in that day's copy of the *Wiener Unabhängige Zeitung*. You soon came home too, laden down with *Nachmarket* shopping like a housekeeper, a surprised look on your face. You put your string bags down and you were about to say something when I thrust your gift at you and said, 'David, I love you,' in a weird tone, like an off-key tenor. I stood there, with your present held out in front of me, waving it at you like a prize fish. When you started to laugh I didn't know what to do. You reached forward, still laughing, took the novel out of my hands, put it on the table, wrapped your arms around me and you said I know, how very nice of me to finally tell you.

Later, after we had made love, I lay on top of you and suggested that perhaps I really should practise telling you I loved you, or else who knew when I would say it again, it could become like that piano in the corner that no one ever plays. You said 'of course, by all means tell me as often as you like, that would be wonderful. But just now could you be a little quiet, because I want to read *Die Aufzeichnungen des Malte Laurids Brigge* and I have to concentrate.

More dreams of you have thrown up the strangest pairings, like a magician's game of pontoon.

Recently you were Olivier wandering Elsinore, small book in hand. You walked and read your battered copy of 'Sonette an Orpheus' and everywhere a voice said, 'But look where sadly the poor wretch comes reading.' And also, sometimes when I dream about you, you run sideways like Chaplin into a strange room full of familiar people. I am standing at the bar. I look at you from across a room like a stranger might, I buy you a drink, I flirt with you but that is all. After a few minutes of bar talk and smoking you suddenly snap out of your role as the beautiful young stranger, you shake your head as if to wake yourself up and then you look at me with the horror of recognition, in your face are a thousand things, surprise, shock, passion. But I won't even kiss you. You want me to. You beg me to but I won't. I stand there, in black tie, and study your every feature. I smoke a cigarette, tears caught in the web of my eyelashes. But I won't touch you. You walk away, and prepare to take a running leap at me from across the room. You want to knock me down, pin me to the floor and kiss me, but you can't move, you have no control. You swear at me in German because it sounds more impressive than it does in English. This has no effect. You rant and rave like a bohemian and there is no response. You pick up things and throw them at me, aspidistras, elephant foot umbrella stands, soda syphons, tennis racquets. They all bounce off me and fall in an untidy mess at my feet.

John.

14th June 1969

Dear Caithleen. Our little girl would have been so much like you say. I would have enjoyed such a child, a child who feigned disregard, who never let me know the true value of her love, but would express it every now and then. We still have the grief. That is the way it should be. And I will leave you with a sadness years deeper. I have no way to make this better. And the sugar of nostalgia, it will not help you. Death will be a bitter pill. You think Claire is the brave one. But you are the brave one, to pluck us out of our English exile, plant us back in Irish soil, to keep the ravens away from my eyes, lungs and heart. Remember, no one came to our wedding day. It's hard to believe this now. But that day there was only you and I and the Dublin priest and his cavernous Catholic

Church. I remember the weight of my wedding ring on my left hand. And hours after our invisible wedding, I sat across from Claire in your Granny's kitchen. Your sister was missing only a Tokarev seven-shot revolver, several sheets of protocols and a scratchy fountain pen. I thought then that Irish women were superior to any *Organi* interrogator, they had their calculated female wrath, a slowly concocted ancestral brew, stewed over generations. She would not leave me alone. She admired me at the press conference, but when I began to express an interest in her beloved sister, she saw me as a murderer, a hypnotist, some Rasputin who had bewitched you, some false Dmitri who would kill you all in your beds. On that flat grey afternoon of our wedding, tired of her interrogation of me over all hours, do you remember, you dragged her through the house and into the front garden, where you yelled, screamed, and bellowed. I watched. I saw that you wanted to slap her hard with your wedding hand, but you were resisting with all your will. James asked me to come away from the kitchen window for a good strong cup of tea. As the voices of sisters flew around the house, cracking the windowpanes and disturbing nesting swallows, James said to me, 'This will all be settled soon, not to worry. And don't be taking anything Claire says to heart, Dmitri – she is always the one to saddle up and ride fast into the fire – that is why we love her.' Yes, that has turned out to be true.

The day is curling away. The dog is resting under the workbench. He is a good dog. We are both tired from working. Don't be concerned. I have eaten a cheddar cheese sandwich, had a cup of tea. The dog has his head in his paws and he is muttering about hares never caught. I am a little agitated. These cigarettes will kill me before my heart does. They are like inhaling thin red arrows. You send that Irish pigeon to Petrograd, the Cheka will conjure it into a cruise missile and send it right back, blow the peat bogs to hell. I am enjoying this writing. You and I, we live through words, they are how we understand the world. For decades now, I have read the work of clever exiles that have taken *samadat* poems and made *tamizdat*; even though Mandelstam in English will always be counterfeit, he tore his own mouth on the Russian words; he bled to death for them. English has been a good language to me, much like a kind elderly uncle, but still I can only dream in Russian. We are so dependent on words, you and I. That is why I love the dog. His world is in his arse, his nose, his tongue, in the pads of his paws. It is not simpler for him, this life, but it is rounder I think, one rolling ball of experience he is constantly chasing, chasing, chasing.

The dog has stopped his boycott. This morning

he walked up the drive to the greenhouse. He loitered in the doorway like an old-fashioned juvenile delinquent. He slunk under the workbench. His ears twitched from the sound of the rock 'n' roll. He watched the radiogram, he watched the record go around and around, and still he could not quite believe what it was he was hearing. These songs on the second record, they are held together with acidic guitars. They are so loud, so funny, so eccentric it seems to me as if Ilf, Petrov, Bulgakov and Zamyatin got very, very drunk one night and formed a rock 'n' roll band. There is a song about revolution that is too slow. There is another song that sounds like Dadaist radio, strips of nonsense making some sense.

And I love him, our dog. He got through the day without growling every time the guitars started to blast, without picking up his paws and leaving in a huff. He thinks I've gone strange in my old age, but we worked together like we used to, he brought me the right brushes, he chewed on the handle of the palette knife a little to form that rough edge I need. He likes Harrison if he likes any of them at all; his tail almost wags when he hears that voice. Today, the painting resembled an anatomical wedding cake. The dog didn't know what to make of it. It isn't the no-colour that bothers him, I can tell that, it is the absence of what remains. He does not know how to look at the painting, and the painting, it does not know how to look at him. I can tell by the way he looks at me he is wondering what I am doing, where all this paint will lead. I may be free from the tyranny of colour but all the other problems remain. What kind of work is this, when you can assume nothing you have done before will ever work for you again? When I step back from the white, the huge canvas, which is not blank, not flat, but has the culture of white cut into it, I have to resist the urge to walk into it, as if it were a world of white, a landscape cold and dangerous and so obviously the North. And I cannot think about home without thinking about Viktor.

Caithleen. For all of these years, this is what I have imagined happened to my brother. Back. Back in 1928 at the apartment on Nevsky Prospect, Viktor sits at his 1906 Odessa Underwood in his section of the room, with a bottle of Altai vodka. There is no one else in the apartment. All the other tenants are out. There is only the sound of his fingers striking the keys. He types only a single paragraph onto the page. Then he kneels by the stove and tears apart four full, thick notebooks. He spends the rest of his evening reading. A little after midnight, the OGPU come to the apartment with the neighbour, Fania Streletsky, as their willing civilian witness. (Fania's face was always the first thing Viktor saw when he unlocked the door and stepped out into the corridor. She kept a card index of everyone's visitors.) They search all of Viktor's papers, looking for new, unpublished stories. The *Organi* take the single white sheet of paper out of the typewriter. They arrest Viktor and slap a large red wax seal on the apartment door. Viktor is put in the back of a Black Maria and taken to Kresti. For three days and three nights Viktor's interrogator allows Viktor no sleep. On the first night, Viktor is shown several of his unpublished short stories. The officer has underlined the anti-Soviet paragraphs with a thick, black pencil. Viktor is accused of reading Zamyatin's novel *We*, and Pilnyak's short novel *Mahogany*. On the second night without sleep, Viktor believes he can hear them beating me in the adjacent room, that he can hear me screaming. On the third night, Viktor signs the already written confession, a fairy tale about his anti-Soviet activities, his constant contact with Trotskyists, his rejection of the Party. Viktor is charged under Article 58. In July 1928, he is transported from Kresti in a Stolypin wagon to Kem, then by boat to the Solovetsky Islands.

Viktor walks up the hill with all the others to the Solovetsky monastery, to the barracks inside the Solovetsky Kremlin, to a place on the broad planks. The political prisoners of '28 are not the politicos of the early twenties; they have no whitewashed cells, no teapots, no sugar cubes, no reading rooms, no lectures, no literary discussions. They fell trees, they haul trees, they cut trees, they make roads. On Solovetsky, in the longest stretches, in the coldest nights, it is nothing against nothing, shadow against shadow, light against light. Viktor places in his mind one word in front of another, laying tracks in the snow one footprint at a time. He inches his way through the night like this every night, every night for almost two years. In the summer of 1930 he stands outside the Solovetsky monastery in new boots. He twists the string that holds together his brown paper package, while he waits for the boat to take him to his exile in Novosibirsk. When he arrives in his Siberian room, Viktor sits at a table with a stolen ballpoint and thin paper and he begins to write. The story he writes, the story I have locked away in my suitcase, it is the story of a man who makes a *tropa* where there is none. A man who walks to the northern edge of the Solovetsky Islands, who walks across the White Sea and into the Arctic Circle, walks over the Barents Sea to the Arctic itself, to a monastery of glaciers. A man so entranced by *severnoye siyanie*, he cannot stop walking. Like Yevtushenko's Charlie Chaplin, he pounds out a tap dance of mortal sadness.

Dmitri.

20th June 1969

Dearest boy. The news of Viktor decades after the event – I had to make myself finish it. And so I have only just come to the end of Akhmatova's words, which you left in the bedroom while I was in the bath this morning. You covered my dusty dressing mirror, the whole long length of the thing, with her words. When Akhmatova came to Oxford in '65, when others went, you couldn't. You couldn't speak to her, you said to me then, because she stayed and bore witness to the terror. Because when a hole had appeared in their coffin-tight logic, you had stepped through, and walked away. I don't know what to say to that, I who have loved you this long. Would I rather you were never there, in London that evening, with your grief and your sorrow flowering around you, would I rather you had died along with millions of others? – no, of course not. But you may wish you had, turning back, looking over your shoulder. How could you not, dear boy. I sometimes believe this is why your heart has become so complicated, the impossibility of living the life that you have, the impossibility of freedom. This morning I stood in the kitchen doorway, reading your letter, while the notorious dog had his cold tea and hot buttered toast. We could hear the rock 'n' roll coming from the greenhouse, which made us miss

'The Goons' and their airwave synaesthesia. We wandered upstairs to the study. I turned the radio on, made myself listen to a news report about more trouble in the North. Then I tuned the radio to the BBC and sat sideways in my favourite armchair, legs draped over the arm like an undergraduate. The dog curled up under my feet. We listened to 'The Jet-Propelled NAAFI' and the dog was all happiness.

As I read your letter, I thought again about that suitcase of yours, the one with Viktor's handwriting locked inside. I leant back in the favourite armchair. I listened to the dog chuckle at 'The Strolling Prime Minister of No Fixed Address'. I let your letter linger in my fingers and I felt a sadness I had not sought but that had found me, there in the deep. The dog and I today, we went walking, as we do, he and I, once a week perhaps, like he is taking me out on a date. We walked down into the village then along to Our Lady's Grotto, then up the hill again so the dog could slink his way through the overgrown paths of the woodlands, the same woods Claire and I used to play in as little girls, Granny's tall tales ringing in our ears. The dog sniffed his way, his nose stuck to the earth, as if he were reading a newspaper. We followed the overgrown path along the old stone wall and went up over the stone steps. We walked across the raised ditch which divides one field from the other; the dog couldn't resist barking at the horses, which were so close to him he could almost jump on them, and at that point he was your dog, not mine. Then we were down and out onto the road. I may be old, but I was still nimble enough. The dog led the way to Barr Aerach. He hummed to himself, some strange dog tune he picked up from O'Brien's border collie. As we turned into the crossroads and we climbed, the view began to reveal itself. Today I did a quick nod to the estuary, to the hills, but as it was a miracle of a day, I looked towards the east end of the village and I could see clear beyond it the wide mouth of the bay, to the long arm of the Old Head of Kinsale, to the skirts of the Atlantic. I felt a strong urge to come back for the car and drive around to the Old Head. I asked the dog what he thought but he was not so interested, the scent of something had caught his attention. So we left the view, your dog and I, as he needed to track the smell that had exploded in his nose, and I only just managed to keep him on the road, he had an almost supernatural urge to break into the fields and find what it was he was looking for. We walked east along the top of the village like circus performers. The beautiful black cows looked up at us occasionally but mostly not. Gorse and whitethorn covered the hedgerows like white wedding gifts. This is happiness, if you ever need to remind me.

We walked, your dog and I, working our way back down to the east end of the village, glimpses of Broadstrand Bay there for us, working our way down and down the road through the woods, spilling out at St John's and both of us in need of a drink. We wandered past The Lifeboat and on to The Sail 'n' Anchor. I sat outside, and sent the dog in. Some time later Barry came out with my Murphy's stout, the dog and a bowl of water. He asked how you were getting on and I said grand, considering your troubles and he said that was fine, that was good. He asked would the fellas be seeing you on Sunday morning after Mass and I said there was no doubt, you would be down as usual, eleven fifteen on the dot. He said there would be a GAA broadcast this Sunday, they'd have the TV on for that and for the pleasure of listening to Michael O'Hehir. I said you would enjoy that for sure. I said I was going to Fiona's after and would he be needing anything at all, and he said no, thanks, the lads were about today, they could go down. He took my two shillings, wiped the table down for me and said he'd best be getting on with things. There was one last pat on the head for the dog and he was gone inside.

Paul Wainwright stopped to say hello – he's shaved his beard off (!) – said he was tired of people thinking he'd come to Ireland for the dole and a tepee. He's keen to drive you up to Dublin to see the William Crozier exhibition sometime soon and I told him you'd like that. He asked how the painting was coming along and I said he should walk up and have a look, you wouldn't mind. I asked him what he was working on and he said some new pieces for the Kilkenny Design Workshop, he'd be up all hours firing for the next month or so, pushing the local electrics. He hoped the lines wouldn't arc too much, but he knew hoping wouldn't stop it from happening. He had to be off though, he had to make a phone call at Fiona's to his brother in Yorkshire. A nice young man, that Paul Wainwright, an excellent eye, good artist's hands, I told him we wanted first look at the ceramics when they are ready. Looking out at the bay, sipping at my stout, the dog's tail thwacking the dirt like a metronome, I thought about our wedding day, our wedding day that was all nothing and no one but ourselves and that Dublin priest, the only sign of celebration that first kiss you gave me once we were married, that kiss into silence. We received the painting not long after. There was a note attached. Packing tape and thick paper gathered around the bottom of the painting like a bride's train. I liked the duck, who you tell me now is not a duck. The bird then. And you, you could hardly believe your eyes. You sent Klee a telegram of poetry. Today at The Sail 'n' Anchor I enjoyed my stout, the dog finished his water. Young Damien gave him a bowl of tepid Barry's tea, the way he likes, and remarked as he scratched the dog behind the ears, that there is nothing sweeter in the world than not having to be anywhere at all. Caithleen.

01/11/11

Hey Lou,

I woke up at five o' clock this morning. I sat on the back step with Crow Bait, sipping Billy Tea and listening to the honeyeaters natter in the pomegranate tree. Three of the Raglan Street Boys were up for a visit, chortling and carolling in their eccentric magpie way. I was re-reading the new postcard I had received from Nate – this one of the Ladies' Entrance, Hotel Woodstock, New York. Discreet marble staircase, Grecian mosaics, heavy dark furniture, someone had written on the back 'Harry and I stayed here on a trip to NY part of the time.' Sitting on the back steps this morning, sipping my tea, listening to the birds, Patrick's lilt drifted through my mind, an old joke of his told down a battered Baghdad telephone: 'Embedded is a strange term for a journo. Makes me feel like a tick on a dog.'

There's a part of the grieving heart that is always turned towards the past. Some days it leans heavily on the body. At seven, I left Hyde Street for Perth. I was leaving early, no need to be at the bookshop until ten. At seven-thirty I walked from Trinity Arcade along Hay Street past the Criterion, down Pier Street past the Playhouse, and onto St George's Terrace. It would have been quicker to nip around the Public Library, but I needed a different walk altogether, a certain rhythm, balanced and considered. In the grounds of St George's Cathedral, as in the rest of the city, there was construction going on. Men in fluoro jackets were landscaping the surrounds and installing floodlights for that new flash sculpture called *Ascalon*. St George's stainless-steel lance pierced a wide, black steel base (the dragon) and surrounding this lance was St George's billowing cloak made of some incredible, indestructible white plastic. I walked around the construction site and up to the front entrance of the cathedral. Inside the doors, sitting at the volunteer desk was an elderly lady called Edna. I walked into the nave. It's difficult to deny God when you are surrounded by such beautiful architecture, the handmade clay bricks, the jarrah beams, the Victorian bluestone, the stained glass, the Italian marble. The building served as a consecrated prism for the pure light that poured into the nave, a light that was my idea of God, a God minus the mythology or the allegory. It was the light that spoke to me through the silence. It was the light that offered me a way forward. On the side of the nave altar, depicted in a relief of carved jarrah, St George leant his body and weapon towards the head of the dragon, the dragon already collapsed and defeated, even in the seconds before the lance was driven into his skull. Once again, as I always had since I was a child, I felt sorry for the dragon – he never seemed very evil to me, more endangered and persecuted. So now I much preferred the post-modern representation outside – evil as a hard, cold, block of darkness that needed to be destroyed by a sharp, clean instrument. I veered away from the altar, to the left of the pulpit, to where the candles were sitting in their metal stand. I unfolded a curled wick with my left thumb and struck a match. You would think that adding another tiny light to that cavernous place would mean nothing, but that wasn't true. I left the light burning and went into the Soldier's Chapel. There were the flags of local regiments, plaques for the decorated and the fallen, a pennant from HMAS *Perth*, the Villers-Bretonneux Cross. This is where I talk to Patrick. I never told you this. I don't know why I am telling you now. I talked to Patrick about Nate, his antique New York postcards. I talked about you, eloquently drunk in Berlin bars.

I talked about Pete, as dependable as the Freo Doctor. I talked about Crow Bait, who now has seventy-eight friends on Facebook. I talked about the city growing fat and fast on the unstoppable mining. I don't know.

So for the last six years, every month or so, I have gone to the place where we held Patrick's memorial service, and within a small chapel for the honoured dead I have whispered to my brother. Now you know. It's a little like returning to the end of your favourite movie without watching the whole thing, it gets tired, and old but you can't seem to stop yourself because a part of you lives in that last few moments of film, you're there now as well, watching the inevitable happen again. Do you know that there is a labyrinth outside the cathedral, it is stencilled into the red brick forecourt between the cathedral and the Public Library. Apparently it's a replica of the labyrinth that exists on the floor of the Chartres Cathedral. In typical Australian fashion, it looks more like some stencilled schoolyard ball game than a spiritual pursuit. Office workers cross over it without a second thought, and of the people I have seen actually walk through it from beginning to end, most seem to be doing it for fun, not for contemplation. Once I got over the thought that the Perth labyrinth looked like some kind of Leunig netball court, I could walk into it and around it without feeling like a complete idiot, you know? I can't say that I pray, or meditate; all I do is walk with the wish to remember Patrick, to not forget him as the years tumble over his death. If he knew I was doing this, he would love me for it and tease me about it at the same time: wasn't he absolutely unforgettable without such silly bloody rituals? Of course, but that doesn't stop me walking in strange sequences, practising my memories of him like some kind of familial rote learning. A bit mad I know, but this is what I do.

This morning I got up from my pew in the Soldier's Chapel and went outside to the labyrinth. A speedy courier on his bicycle shot across its white paint, veered right through the walkway and disappeared into Hay Street. It would have been about a quarter to nine. Office workers hurried through the forecourt to their posts with coffee cups and muffins from Croissant Express. And I entered the labyrinth. It is not like a maze. There is only one way in, and one way out. You have to be mindful to not overstep the painted lines, as the pathways are narrow. As you enter the labyrinth there is an involuntary uplift in your lungs, as if you were taking flight, it's strange, but this has happened to me every time I have entered. The sensation is more physiological than mystical, more a consequence of the physical map than of any spiritual secrets being revealed. But still. This morning when I entered the labyrinth I saw eight-year-old Patrick, bright and blond with eyes of hazel like Dad; wearing his pride and joy, those white Dunlop Volleys; a Patrick not quite jumping and not quite skipping, doing something almost in between and quintessentially Patrick. And then I saw Buster beside him, looking up at Patrick, lovesick. I don't think I ever told you, but Buster was our first dog, a fox terrier/ Jack Russell cross with the brains of a canary and the stamina of a fast pack rat. Buster's motto was, 'Why walk when you can throttle?' Seeing the boy and his dog together, I remembered there was an old family story about Buster, a story that had been dropped from the family repertoire sometime in the late eighties; so you haven't heard it. One Saturday morning during the summer of '78 Buster got out. Someone (probably Pete on his way to schoolboy cricket) had left the side gate open and he was gone before Dad could finish swearing. Patrick and I were dispatched on our Malvern Stars to go get the little bastard. We rode, we looked, we called from atop our low-rider saddles, 'Buster! Here boy!' but there was no Buster to be seen, or heard. After searching all of Buster's usual hidey holes, after riding up and down the cross streets surrounding our house (Wasley, Forrest, Alma, Raglan, Grosvenor, Chelmsford) Patrick and I decided that Buster had done the unthinkable – he had crossed Vincent Street and entered Hyde Park. We sprinted down Hyde Street then jumped off our bikes at the edge of Vincent knowing Dad would know (somehow he'd know) if we rode across such a busy road. We crossed the road with care, jumped back on our bikes and swung them down into the park, calling Buster's name. It was an adventure now.

I heard Buster's bark first and took off in chase of it, Patrick following as fast as his little-brother legs could pedal. Buster wasn't that easy to find, his bark seemed to run in circles around us but we couldn't actually see the dog himself. I tried to follow the sound of it but I kept jumping the gun, seeing Buster in every small mutt that passed us, even though they all had leads and owners. I very nearly collided with a young woman and her pure-bred Jack Russell. Then Patrick stood up on his bike, pointed and shouted. There, in the middle of the largest of the two ponds, on the scraggly Huck Finn island, was Buster, barking his head off as every single duck that had been nesting on the island swam away from it and its newest inhabitant. 'Oh Christ,' I muttered in a perfect imitation of my father. As we cycled closer, we could see that Buster had absolutely no clue how to get back to dry land, it was as if the swim to the island had dazzled his little brain so much he had no grey cells left to work out how to get back. He barked and barked and barked. Soon, he would whine, then howl. Patrick and I leapt off our bikes and half-threw them on the grass. I took off past the spot where Buster was barking. Patrick followed, yelling at me, 'Whaddya doing?' and I replied, 'Finding the shortest way over, you drop kick!' Patrick ran after me then I suddenly stopped. I'd found a place where the distance to the island couldn't have been more than half the length of Beatty Park pool. I could do that with my eyes closed. Luckily there was a good amount of water in the pond, I could avoid the evil mud as long as I didn't touch the bottom. I slid into the water, my mouth firmly closed, my head as high above the water as I could manage. I breast-stroked my way through alarmed ducks while Patrick called out Buster's name. Just as I got to the edge of the island Buster came tearing into view and without breaking stride the dog leapt over my head and into the water, making straight for his beloved Patrick. I swore very loudly, turned around and followed the crazy mutt back to shore. When I got there Patrick had Buster by the collar and the dog was shaking himself, spraying Patrick with dirt and mud and water. 'The lead?' Patrick asked me, as I was climbing up the bank and out of the water. I shook my head slowly. No lead.

*

I was at the centre of the labyrinth.

As I began to walk back the way I had come, I thought of Patrick's battered old white cowboy hat, the one I wear on impossibly sunny days when the heat gets too much for me. I feel more like Buck Jones than Lucinda Williams (and you tease me about it) but it is Patrick's hat so I wear it, you know? He got it in Nashville. When he came home to Perth he told me a story about falling in love with a girl in a band, he told me not to tell anyone, falling in love was not really his style, he didn't want anyone to know. But he was so close to it he said to me, so close that he could hear the whispers of a new life as he walked into the bar each night to listen to this girl sing. It didn't help that she looked like a young Emmylou Harris, the spitting image of the girl on the cover of *Elite Hotel.* Hell, more than half the room was in love with her. Patrick never spoke to her, just put handwritten notes in the tip jar along with several fifty-dollar bills. There were other notes floating around in that jar, of various colours, shapes and sizes. The girl didn't wear a wedding ring, she didn't seem to be going out with any of the boys in her band. On his last night in Nashville, Patrick and his battered white hat stayed on after the gig was over. He leant against the bar with his hands in his pockets, looking like he'd lived in Nashville all his life, thanks to his good

West Australian stock – didn't matter he'd never been near a horse in his life, his forbears had and there they all were in his stance and his attitude, putting on a show for the girl on the stage. He knew she was going to break his heart, but he didn't care. If only she would speak to him. When the stage was clear, and the band was packed up, she came over to the bar with a couple of the players. He said hello, she asked him where he got his accent. He told her. She asked him to tell her something about the place. He did. So he came from the desert, was that right she asked him. He said no one came from the desert, no white man anyway, we clung to the edges of our country and learnt to live with what the desert meant. We were always looking for the next horizon he said, the next place. That's why you like the songs, she said to him, because in this music we're all travelling. He guessed she was right. He said to her that he was leaving in the morning but should he stay? She smiled and said no, there was no reason. He bought her a whisky, then said goodnight. Patrick left the bar that night the happiest man in Nashville – he'd just been in a country-and-western song.

When I regained the entrance to the labyrinth I looked up at the brick cathedral in front of me, the flag of St George flying from its tower, a single spire jaunting into the air. And close, quite close, were the office buildings of international banks, and there, just there, the cool dark glass of the Exchange Plaza, the ASX numbers running around the outside of the building. I looked up, and the numbers didn't mean a thing to me. If Patrick had been with me, he would have looked up at those numbers, and the numbers that came along after them, and he could have told me a story, a story about the city, and the companies nestled in the city, drawing in their vast profits from their operations up north and offshore, making those numbers move and shake, which in turn was building another city within the old city, a city of glass and steel within the beauty of a handmade cathedral.

I don't know, though – Pete also used to say that it was only Patrick's self-deprecating humour that saved him from being an out-and-out prick. I have to admit that was true – I used to say as much myself, before he died, you heard me many times say such things about him. And not only that, but he was so bloody elusive, like a celebrity passing through his hometown, he never seemed to stay long. Did you get sick and tired of Patrick's journo bragging, all those bloody stories of presidents, dictators and political dissidents? I did. Pete, well, Pete just ignored Patrick's fat tales and got on with brewing his beer. Pete was happy to see his brother whether he'd just returned from Kuwait or from the corner deli. Most of all we loved him.

When we were told Patrick's body was finally coming home I wanted to say to the Consulate staff, can't you bring his body back overland, then by boat to Western Australia. Then we would have a month, one month of imagining the long, slow journey, one month to understand that he was coming home to us. But no, his body arrived twenty-three hours after it had left Iraq. We had less than a day. I remember the young female official walking towards Pete and me, carrying Patrick's battered old suitcase, carrying Patrick's suit zipped up in its black protector; and we took Patrick's things from her, we took them like Patrick was coming along later. You have to understand this, and I know you've tried to, but let me make it plain. There's a dark, dark tunnel that runs through my heart, it was carved out when Patrick died and if I get on a plane this tunnel will collapse and wreck me. All of my dreams, they are dreams of trains, buses, cars, ships and trucks. In my dreams I buy a sturdy raincoat for travelling, a new suitcase, a watch. I travel through landscapes foreign and domestic, I travel alone and without you, on the way to you or from you, I travel without conversation or the serendipity of strangers. I don't speak to anyone. There is meditation in the sound of the train on tracks, the car on gravel, the ship on the sea, it is all forward momentum but without beauty, or purpose or passion. I travel like a disinterested politician, engaged everywhere and so engaged with nothing and with no one. My passport is fake, my travel documents forged, but in the nostalgic world of my dreams these things are still possible to get away with, to be almost someone else going to somewhere else. It is a little like I imagine death to be. I've just read Rilke's only novel, *The Notebooks of Malte Laurids Brigge*. In the book, Brigge remarks that in the old days, people knew that they bore their own death within them like the stone within the fruit. As if our lives were spent growing our own deaths inside of us, as if that was what life was actually for, and nothing else. My brother is gone but gone where, I can't say. That's the most maddening part. To not know where he is, when the world is without him and wants him back, makes nothing final. Grace.

20th November 2011

Grace. We're in London. It's very late. I want to read some of your poetry books. Some Mary Oliver or Rilke, some Andrew Motion or cuddly Simon Armitage. Earlier in the night Stow did Graham Norton, now we're hiding in the back of his favourite shabby booze den. Anyone recognises him and wants to get to him, there's a chorus line of large gentlemen seated in front of us. I am drinking tea by the way. Stow is drinking whisky and reading *Vagabond Holes*. Three more nights in London then we're all around the country. I keep running into Australians. Natalie K. is at the same hotel with that skinny-tie husband of hers. Lewis sent me an email just to say hello and it turns out we'll be in Liverpool at the same time. Bob came up from Brighton in a rattling old Ford Anglia straight out of Harry Potter. He tells me Cage is still in Nashville working with the twins but they all want to come home to Perth, play some gigs at Mojo's, the Fly By Night. Small rooms for old friends. We both got a little nostalgic about my old days running with the band, it's hard not to but what's gone is gone. It's been gone a long time now. Stow and I had tickets last night to Emily Barker and the Red Clay Halo. He had a chat with Emily after the show. They knew each other in Perth. Emily told Stow that he writes like Dylan, and he said nah he didn't, he was more like a David McComb – scribbling in all the cramped and grubby places.

Later. Now I'm in my hotel room listening to Tame Impala, trying to conjure up other voices from home here in this beautiful and gloomy subterranean city. It was lovely to speak with you the other day. I hear the sound of your voice and something starts up in me again. Something I put away while I'm travelling. Something so essential to me I can almost overlook it. After Patrick's death what we lost were his constant messages and updates, the stream of data that was Patrick, which held together your love for him until the day he arrived home for a visit, larger than life, unexpected. And after he died there was the absence of these messages, making it difficult for you to breathe. I could see that but I didn't know what to do for you, and I'm sorry. Without you in the room with me, everything I say to you is false. Grief never really dies, it is the mirror cracked, the house burnt down. I think I understand why the Buddhists insist on the contemplation of death. How else can we be real in the world? Not that I will do it, and neither will you, we'll leave that to those more equipped. Like everyone we know, we'll stay stressed, and tired, and a little bewildered. Perhaps (and please don't be mad at me for saying this) but it's like you believe that Patrick is coming back. He was always away, always leaving, why should his death be any different? I'm sorry if this hurts but this is our problem now. Six years on, it's gone beyond grief and turned into melancholy, into something unworkable, into something which has taken over everything. Even us. Louise.

June 11th '48

Dearest David,

Viv sleeps, curled up on the sofa like Sherlock Holmes. A newspaper is barely in reach of her fingertips, a book is tucked under her feet like a pair of slippers. Viv sleeps and shadows move across her face, nocturnal compositions. Her eyelashes tremble with electricity. She won't wake. The rumblings of distant celebrations, the shouting and the singing, they won't disturb her. It is eleven-thirty in the evening, a cold clear night, and the West Cliff bowling club has been hosting a dance since seven. The past is here in her party dress, picking up the ashtrays, flicking through the magazines, studying the paintings on the wall, stirring a cup of tea with my grandmother's best teaspoon. She sings songs I can barely remember: popular Viennese tunes, Kabarett, vaudeville, music hall. The future is waiting outside, such a young man. He smokes and hits the heel of his muddied shoe against the hard red brick, impatient, slightly too sure of himself. He can't quite gather the composure to come inside and ask her to dance, but he will. Viv sleeps.

She is re-reading *The Big Sleep*. She has always liked Marlowe, a man who talks in Morse code, who reads people as if they were riddles, dangerous ciphers that aren't what they appear to be. But for now, Viv has been lulled into rest by reading. She's fallen into the arms of the settee so correctly I don't know if I ever want to wake her. Viv finds me some nights curled up on the landing. When she sees me there, she kneels down, puts her hand on my left knee and says, 'Johnny, I'm going to make the tea now.' Without opening my eyes, I ask her in German if she could tell me the way to the Rummelhardtgasse because I am new to Vienna, and I have already lost my way several times now. Vivienne replies in English, 'Yes, of course, nothing simpler, perhaps some tea before you go on your way.' I say, in German, yes that would be lovely, thank you. Sometimes, I ask her for directions to the Rummelhardtgasse apartment. Several times I have been so overcome with emotion I don't ask her anything, but even then I'm struggling to find a way to get to someplace else. Vivienne says if one day I work out where it is I want to go, I'll take off like the Swedes trying for the four-minute mile.

It is eleven forty-nine. As the revels have died down to a dull roar, I have put on the Bournemouth Symphony Orchestra BBC recording of Beethoven's Piano Concerto No. 4 in G Major Opus 58. Mother is the soloist. This particular concerto was my mother's fourth child, her most difficult and her most rewarding. Viv can't hear it without crying, so I am glad she is fast asleep (this is a woman who can sleep through a bombing raid; to her, Beethoven is merely a butterfly). None of Mother's children were musical. Not because we didn't care for the music. But by the time we were seven or eight, by the time we had seven or eight years of Mother's relentless regime of practice and performance, we understood what great music demanded, and to us it seemed to be the most serious adult pursuit that existed. Father had his work, but there was another father as well (particularly in Bournemouth), a father of coconut shies and roller-skating. Mother migrated during my early life from Mozart to Beethoven, until she became singularly dedicated to the Master.

I remember this piano concerto in particular, as it was the one that Mother hated and loved with an intensity that was frightening to this small boy. One rare summer Sunday, I was left alone with Grandmother. Father had talked Mother into a walk along the promenade while Alistair and Viv played on the beach with Nanny. I stole the score from my mother's desk. I spread it out on the floor, being careful to keep the pages in their proper order. I can still see the script of Opus 58, the complicated humanity of the Allegro Molto, the impenetrable nature of the notes, then and now. The notes frightened me, but what frightened me more was that my mother could make sense of them, and I had no idea how. That childhood terror of my mother's talents faded with age, but never completely disappeared. When I play my mother's BBC recording of the fourth piano concerto, I usually follow on with Clara Haskil's 1946 performance with the London Philharmonic; her first recording with Decca. If I play one woman and then the other, then my grief can be contained, then the notes are just notes, the harmonies just harmonies, the themes merely themes; nothing more than Beethoven's genius coming through twentieth-century fingers. But tonight, I may not make it through the Allegro Moderato.

In June of '43, several weeks after Mother's death, Mrs Halligan was working in the kitchen. For reasons that are unclear to me, as well as our conversation I remember several unremarkable things. She was mixing up a ginger and date cake. There was a Hunt Pie baking in the oven. There were potatoes on the stove. Blue hydrangeas requisitioned from Cherry Blossom Lane had been arranged in a vase on the kitchen table. To my mind it was a waste of Mrs Halligan's valuable time to have her cook and clean for me alone and I came into the kitchen to broach the subject with her. Southampton evacuees had been billeted in hotels and boarding houses for almost three years; they were no longer being put up in private homes as they had been in '39 and '40. She knew the conversation was coming. I looked at her and realised she wasn't much younger than me; in fact, we could be the same age. She bossed me like I was her oldest son, but really we would have been born a few years apart at the most. Without looking up from her mixing, she asked if I minded her taking a look at the gramophone collection. I said no, of course not, play what you like, and it was then I realised she meant my mother's music. I stood in the doorway with my hands in my pockets, not wanting to say what needed to be said.

Then Mrs Halligan spoke first. She said – 'That first young pilot buried in the East Cemetery, you might remember he died in a flying accident in November '39. Not long after, the morning of December 11th, Harold and I were told we had lost both our boys the night before, another aeroplane accident, it was. As soon as we were told, the minute after, I took my hat and my coat and walked straight to St Peter's. I walked down the aisle, and sat in the third pew and there I stayed. For hours and hours, no one approached me, no one asked me to leave. Harold came just before the blackout, with a torch and some blankets and cushions, he slept lying on the pew, but I didn't sleep. The next day, people brought food, sandwiches and the like. Harold thanked them but I wouldn't eat a thing. And on the third day, your mother came. She'd brought vegetable broth, still warm from this stove, and bread spread with half a week's ration of butter. Everyone else had left their food, they set it down on the pew or gave it to Harold, but your mother came and sat next to me. She served us both. And we ate soup, in the church, not saying a word.'

Mother was walking past Beales the Sunday afternoon of the bomb raid. She had well and truly retired from public performance before the war, but once hostilities began, and the numbers of the BSO were quickly reduced by half and then dwindled to twenty-four by 1940, she felt she had no choice but to resume playing again. And she still played beautifully, some would argue she was at her best in those years. That Sunday afternoon Mother was out and about on her standard pre-performance ramble, she loved to walk through the town towards the Pier Front Baths, then turn up onto the West Cliff.

While others went up there for goofing – to watch the dog fights from the cliff tops – Mother went up for other reasons. She would look beyond the barbed wire, the gaping hole in the Pier, the swarm of aircraft. She would stand above the West Beach and look at the Pier, then beyond to Boscombe and the ghost of Hengistbury Head, then to the Needles blazing white. She never tired of that view.

That Sunday evening, two hours after the bomb raid which killed so many, which destroyed Beales and the Metropole Hotel, the Bournemouth Symphony Orchestra played their scheduled performance. What was to be a celebration of their fiftieth anniversary became a memorial service for the dead. Tonight, up at the bowling club, they would almost be through the beer and the Bournemouth 'champagne', and I hope Mrs Halligan is dancing with Mr Halligan. I hope she manages to waltz her way through memories of her boys. I hope that she closes her eyes and prays, holding on to her husband as they glide, praying for things to be better now, for things to be alright. And I hope it comes true. Viv sleeps. It is after midnight and the past, tired of waiting, has draped her wrap over her pretty shoulders and gone outside to flirt with the future, to ask him for a cigarette. She knows he really is an awkward boy, not a grown man, and she will make allowances for this.

John.

June 12th–15th '48

Dear David,

On the afternoon of June 11th, Viv asked me, as she sipped her tea and looked out at the persistent rain, whether I was planning to resurrect the tennis court. I said I hadn't thought of it, no one had played on it for over ten years. 'It's such a pity,' she said. I told Viv that you saw Gottfried von Cramm play his first international tournament in 1929, at the Blau-Weiss Club in Berlin. Lacoste won the title, but von Cramm beat several very good players. And, of course, you and I listened to the greatest match ever played, von Cramm at the height of his powers, the Davis Cup Interzone Final, '37, against Don Budge. Vivienne came away from the doors and brought her tea cup to the table. It was Viv who had read it in the papers about von Cramm, his arrest by the Gestapo in '38, and it was she who told me once I found my way back home. I realise now that he was arrested just days before the *Anschluss*. He was never sent to a camp. After prison, he survived the Russian Front. These past few years he's been rebuilding the Rot-Weiss Club and he's the number-one German tennis player again, in his late thirties. Vivienne looked out at the neglected tennis court. 'It wouldn't be Wimbledon, but we could have a good playing surface again, if it stops raining.'

That Davis Cup match in '37, Carter and Lawrence were there. As we listened to the broadcast in our little apartment in Vienna, I could not imagine the Swastika flying over Wimbledon, Queen Mary taking tea with Nazi Reichssportführer Hans von Tschammer und Osten. But the match! Once the match started, nothing else mattered. Once von Cramm strode out onto the court at 4.30pm all other concerns melted away. His proclivities were the worst-kept secret in Berlin, we were all amazed that he was still playing for the Third Reich. But what a matinee idol, rich, charming, married to his sporting sweetheart, articulate, a gentleman on the court and off, no wonder the Nazis held him up to be the epitome of true Aryan manhood. Pity for them he was a queer.

So I told Vivienne yes, that I would investigate restoring the tennis court. Viv thought that was marvellous. She took it as a sign of progress, like my walking. She didn't know there were no signs, that there was no optimism attached to these ideas, only their counterweight against grandfather's old revolver. On June 13th, Viv telephoned Richmond Tennis Club and asked the groundskeeper for his advice. He gave her the name of a new book – *Turf* – a guide to the restoration of lawns, courts, and golf runs neglected during the war. Viv marched me out the front door of the Red Villa and into town. We carried with us the idea of the day, and the promise of tennis. We went to the book counter at Brights and bought two copies of *Turf*. Viv borrowed a copy of *Kerry's Directory* and wrote down the telephone number of 'Henry and Henry Ltd, Landscape Gardeners and Contractors'.

She mentioned to me that Richmond and West Hants were looking for new members, or for old members to rejoin, not that there were many who could afford it. She asked if I'd like to play again. I said we'd see. A social game perhaps. I could see her organising it in her mind, a fine afternoon, Richmond Tennis Club, Victoria Avenue. Viv suggested tea while we were at Brights. I asked her to order something for me. I was going for a quick walk. I walked out of the department store and down to the Central Gardens. There is something about the anonymity of the walking man. Sometimes the only time I can have you, fully in my body and at the front of my heart, is when I am alone and walking fast. When there is no one standing in front of me I have to lie for, or make comfortable. All those years we had together, we had not realised that what the public really loathes in homosexuality is not the thing itself but having to think about it. Several months after we met, I left Barts early to attend the Sexual Reform Congress at Wigmore Hall. I was not a member of the WLSR, or the BSSSP, so I sat at the back of the hall in the dead head seats, with the reporters and the local feminists and the common garden gawkers. There had been a strong emphasis on homosexual rights at the 1926 Berlin Congress. Two years later, Magnus Hirschfeld had read Kurt Hiller's pro-rights speech in Copenhagen. Perhaps for these reasons, at Wigmore Hall, homosexual rights had for the most part disappeared off the agenda. Papers were given on eugenics, birth control, marriage reform, censorship, and psychoanalysis. After his paper on Marriage Counselling, I introduced myself to Magnus Hirschfeld and shook his hand. I wanted to ask for his help. But I didn't. Instead, Hirschfeld and I had a fifteen-minute discussion on the psychological and sociological training of doctors in order to assist them in their consultations with married couples. Then I thanked him for his time. I refused all the literature offered to me on my way out. I didn't stop to look at the books they were selling in the foyer. I went back to work. Back to Barts. Back to my white coat and stethoscope.

On my Bournemouth walk from Brights, I followed the Bourne Stream, its signature winding its way through the gardens, to the war memorial. There, guarding the stone steps were two marble lions, one sleeping, one roaring. Two men from the council stood on the steps quietly discussing the cleaning of the memorial, in particular the lions. Wreaths and flowers covered the base of the Doric column. The men from the council moved away from the memorial towards the Town Hall, still whispering about their brief, their fingernails clipped and short, their moments quick and precise, their decisions kept firmly under their hats.

I walked up the stone steps past the lions and stood in front of the column. On the column, far above the First War dedication, there's a new plaque dedicated to the men and women of the County Borough of Bournemouth who gave their lives in the 1939–1945 War. Built in 1922, the memorial was designed, like so many others, to be a Temple of Memory. I stood there, as I have many times before, and I thought about the boys who had died in my hospital, under my care; about Mother, Mrs Halligan's boys, and you. I stood there, for some time, and felt nothing but the earth's indifference to the dead. I walked back to Gervis Place, a little disorientated. There was a small plate of lemon curd sandwiches and a tepid cup of tea waiting for me in Brights tearooms. Over that cup of tea Vivienne bullied me into going to Richmond Tennis Club to play a social game, my first game of tennis in over a decade.

So June 14th we wandered through the clubhouse (my name still on the Championship board for 1922–1924). My old tennis clothes hung from me like baggy elephant skin, I looked all of my forty-eight years in them. I'd brought three of my old racquets, one Wilson and two Dunlop. Don Budge used Wilson racquets that day in '37 against von Cramm, pure white racquets made of ash, with sanded wooden handles. By then, no one was using wooden handles anymore, except Budge and Bill Tilden. I hated the leather handles when I first tried one, the leather absorbed so much sweat I had to rip it up to get a better grip. Von Cramm used Dunlop Maxply racquets that afternoon, and as he and Budge walked out onto centre court, he tossed one into the air. The racquet fell on the smooth. Von Cramm would serve. I said to Viv I could play right-handed if she wished, like I used to when we were children, and Vivienne laughed. 'I've had practice, dear brother. The Chap loves this game as much as you do.' Some practice. I did not know that Viv's first serve had improved one hundred per cent, I did not know that she had developed a back-hand game Suzanne Lenglen would have killed for. I thought I had a plan. I thought to myself, Vivienne's first serve is actually a solid second serve, so I should take it on the rise, hit a return deep and then rush the net. But when Viv served, my shoulders rushed forward over my body and my legs couldn't keep up. I was too slow to bring my racquet up to the ambling ball – the result being that the return shot was not deep but so weak that my dear sister smashed it down my backhand line, bringing up chalk dust – 15-love. I won't continue with the Colonel Brand commentary.

As the match progressed, the muscles in my legs began to ring like alarm bells. I'd started out sipping Earl Grey tea but by the middle of the second set I had to pour a jug of water over my head. Vivienne was accommodating, but she knew I didn't need sympathy; I needed a bloody good thrashing and she gave it to me: 3-6, 6-8, 3-6. What happened to my game? Imagine Big Bill Tilden having one of his famously raucous nights out with Tallulah Bankhead in the London Clubs. Being the teetotaller that he is, all he has had to drink all night is glass after glass of water. Imagine that Bill, after barely two hours sleep, wakes up on a bright, crisp summer's morning, rolls into a practice session with Frank Hunter and finds to his horror that he remembers nothing whatsoever about tennis; it has completely disappeared from his body. That's almost what happened to me. After my disgrace, we went home and I dragged out the old wrought-iron garden furniture from the potting shed. Viv brought out from the house a large carafe filled with lemon barley water, and two highball glasses. We sat together, in the early afternoon sun, watching nothing happen on our grandmother's tennis court. On July 20th 1937, when the most beautiful tennis match of the century finally ended after three hours and five sets, no one could quite believe it. Von Cramm vs Budge: 8-6, 7-5, 4-6, 2-6, 6-8. Thousands stayed, afterwards. They stood, they sat, they walked around. They looked at the empty court where the miracle had just occurred. You and I, listening in with the rest of the world, we were there with them. We are there still. John.

22nd June 1969

Dearest Caithleen. The pub fellas, they have heard me speak Russian when I am excited, or drunk, or angry. My mother tongue burns under my English words like hot coals under cracking wood. This has not failed to unnerve your Corkman. We had so much bloody trouble convincing these Republicans that I was Russian and not Communist. Some were very sure (for years and years and years) that the Soviet blockade of the Republic's entry into the UN was down to me. During our early summers here I had to make many telephone calls to polite young Englishmen. The SIS dished up quiet suggestions like marriage guidance. When the local grumblers and gossip mongers saw that there was nothing real to tie their lies together, I think they moved on to other stories – the Dublin journeys of Mary Mead, the night-time cycling of Mr McCreedy, the suddenly wealthy Decklin Drogue. It may have taken thirty-five years, but here I am, and no one has any trouble with me anymore. The fellas down at The Sail 'n' Anchor still rib me and still tell me to 'go and get on to Siberia', the coldest place in the village. And there is nothing else to do even after all this time but stand in the sawdust, drink my stout, and be affectionately bludgeoned (once again).

Caithleen, you love argument. You do not know, but when you invite people to visit you, I like to spy a little, to look at the historian's shoes, the priest's cassock, or the journalist's pen. My only visitors these days are those young painters from the West. They arrive here, now and then, like some small religious cult. They all have ancient cars, and the same neglect of their appearance, or sometimes they have the cut of geologists or academics. These are the young men. The women are different altogether. You have seen them. You have remarked on them, the young women, so beautifully dressed, who bring me cakes and flowers, fresh milk and vegetables. These lovely young women, they look like they are on their way to a great, serious, important meeting in Cork city, when they are only coming along the road to see me. I understand why you clear out when the male painters come up the drive, why you stay in your study or take your bicycle down into the village. These men, they arrive with handshakes and money grumbles, some existential swearing, and they look for cake, or tea, or an offer of the pub. If it is winter and, as Heinrich Böll says, the rain is 'absolute, magnificent and frightening', the brave ones come up the steep drive like the last men in the world. They shake off the ordinary terror of the journey from the Beara or the Sheep's Head. And their first hour of talk, it is full of ordinary tales of your man there (death) cheated. Sometimes they stay, downstairs in the small room with the dog lying in their door (and you have to feed them, I am sorry). Sometimes they try to go home in the devil's weather and they have to come back half an hour later. They laugh at their own idiocy, then the national prayer, it spills out of them like contentment – when God made time, he made plenty of it.

We don't talk about art in the abstract way. We talk like hunters, or soldiers, or explorers, locked into spit and blood. We are losers of sleep, dancers with fatigue, we drag our soiled and sorry bodies through time while the white canvas says nothing, not one word. So we compare wounds and compass bearings. Sometimes, in the forge of conversation, they wait for me to tell them; but they are not old enough to realise I don't have the answer. Nano Reid, she still writes from Drogheda, and Norah McGuinness from Rathmullan (dear Elizabeth Rivers gone now these four years) my companions from those times almost long ago now (the Wertheim Gallery, the Leicester Galleries, the White Stag Group, the Irish Exhibition of Living Art). I don't know what Nora and Nano make of my short, terse notes, I am not inclined to write well to anyone but you, I never have in all my life. You are my friend in the way that Viktor was my friend. He and I, we would talk about anything and everything as we wandered through St Petersburg, over the canals, looking at the world and those within it. We were together. I left half of my heart with him, half of my mind, perhaps the better parts of me, only you could judge.

When I arrived in France, as I have told you many times (forgive these old recountings), Paris was a fancy palace with no money, and no air. When I went to Germany, Klee let me stay with him and his wife and child Felix in Dessau, but I slept too much, drank too much, and wandered around the Bauhaus. It was as if my bones had been left behind with my brother. So this is how I ended up in London, the least favourite city of all the exiles (and so the most anonymous) where I faded into the grey and began to paint. But I was like a man who could only turn in one direction, and so my life came, over time, to consist of ever tightening circles of desperate activity. Then you came. You pulled me sideways, wrenched me out of my Dante wandering.

You took me home. To my surprise even today, I look around me see that I have a life. There is the cup of tea you made me this afternoon, half-drunk and now cold. There is the radiogram still alive and warm but silent. There is the dog sleepy and sighing, stretched out on the floor. And there is this painting, this great whale I began to chase over two years ago now, my great monster that needs the care and attention of a small child so he may live and breathe.

And over my shoulder (if I care to look) are the estuary, and the bay. The warm waters of the Gulf Stream wash in with the absolute cold of the Atlantic; blending with winter rain, the dark pages. I have always worked in the summer, we always came here so I could paint in the summer. In the winter, the autumn, I am drawing, sketching and making notes. You understand why I do this. Others do not understand. There is nothing in the winter world for me to make something out of, but many disagree, and they tell me so. What you could do, Dmitri Palovich, they say, and have said for thirty or more years now, what you could do with the intensity of Ireland in the winter. But you and I know: I wish to do nothing with it. You and I know that I need light. A certain kind of light. I can't say what it is, I have never been able to say what it is. But I know when it is here, when it has arrived here, like the guillemots and razorbills that come to the Old Head every summer. It is here, now, in the strangest times, it comes and goes with the spring rain but I see it, running over the earth faster than anything with blood and muscle. They may be old, but my eyes are trained. I have been looking for the first sign of this light for years, and I know it like my brother. It is here (again) and so I paint.

I may not have another painting in me, and this one, it will take at least another year to finish. The spine of the thing, the vertebrae, that travels down the centre of the painting, done last summer – it has taken these last six months to dry. Now I attempt a first pass at the long tendrils that sprout out of the vertebrae – that wander across the pure white of the painting like calcium ivy. This is delicate, calculating work. It makes the dog nervous. He much prefers it when I attack a painting, when I punch it with the brush or the knife. He can cheer me on in those cases, wag his tail in his enthusiasm. When I work across the face of this painting, when I slowly construct a long, fluid line across its white ground, he knows he has to be quiet, he knows he has to be still, and it is so far from his true being it is almost impossible for him to do this for longer than an hour at a time. So I send him to you, or to the Barry boys in the village, or to Fiona's for the

Cork Examiner, where he will get love and a treat from Fiona's kitchen. I know in his heart he would prefer to stay, to see out the long day with me until it is time for our early evening walk; but I would rather he was happy, not so bound to his loyalty to me all the time. A dog needs a life after all. So, the painting. That was a kindly joke of yours the other evening, that we would have to turn the greenhouse into a gallery, that there was no way we could get the painting out of here, and into a lorry and on to Clonakilty, or Kinsale, or Cork, or Dublin. You weren't sure, but you suspected the painting was too long for any gallery wall in this country. I know you're right, but I had measured the thing before I began, and I said it would fit the space that I had imagined for it. Though when you asked me where that space was, I did not say!

Yours, Dmitri.

25th June 1969

My dearest Dmitri. Years ago I heard a saying that we all eventually end up half a mile from where we started off. I think I believe it now. Yesterday afternoon I finally took the car, left you and the dog to the long white painting, and drove around the bay, past the beaches at Garretstown and Garrylucas. On the way to the Old Head I had to stop the car on the steep road for a line of milkers. The very last cow had horrific mastitis, her udder had blown up like a carnival balloon and she had trouble keeping up with the herd. There was no mercy for her from the farmer, as she was holding everyone up, he was waving his hat at her, shouting, he would push her on until she was over the road with the others, and he could shut the gate behind them. I was sorely tempted to have a word with him, but I could hear my grandfather's voice in my ear, telling me to leave the poor young fella alone, the life of the dairy was hard enough work without some woman getting soft about a dumb animal. So I waited.

There were walkers, of course, winding their way up to the Old Head in the bluster, with sticks and knapsacks, folks from Ballinspittle, a pod of tourists from Kinsale, a pair of Dutchmen from the village. I felt soft driving up in the car, but I knew the walk from the watchtower to the lighthouse would be enough for the likes of me. Even with your troubles (and against all advice) – you would have rubbed salt on your hands and run up the hill with the dog on your back, but you are from the Arctic after all. As a young girl of sixteen I hauled and stacked full butter boxes ready to leave the Dunbar Street creamery, while my brothers laughed and looked on. Today, if they had been here to laugh I would have walked all the way from Garrylucas, but instead I was alone, and there was the car. So I drove on up the hill, I parked the car, the watchtower in the long grass at my back. Walking down towards the Old Head I had a strange urge to make my home there on its cliffs, to live off mussels, salmon, prawns, and at night to sleep inside the old watchtower and never go home, never come home to you. And for a moment I wanted this only if I could be the only one, the only one here, but almost immediately that seemed selfish to me, nothing but pure selfishness and greed. No one could own such a place. (And if one man does, he has let the world in.)

Out on the Head today, there were plenty of folk, being with God Himself, walking and dreaming awake beneath the wide blue sky. When I was a little girl, only eight or nine or so, I thought the Old Head was a great sleeping green whale, its head burrowed into the land, its gigantic tail spread out into the sea. I thought that one day, while I walked towards the wide sea, the whale would wake, the tail would rise and send me flying into the icy waters of Holeopen Bay, east or west of the Old Head, no one would know until it was almost too late. Then those brave young men from the village, they would launch the village lifeboat and row out to find me by some miracle still alive. I would be given whisky and warm things, the boys would sing all the way back to Barry's Point, where Granny would be waiting with boy and horse.

And so the Old Head would become the whale it actually was, it would wrench its large head out of the land at Lispatrick, then dive down and down and down into the sea, flicking off the shell of the Napoleonic watchtower, the ruins of the De Courcey castle, and the lighthouse, like the bloody nuisances they were. I am much older now, and no longer dream of rescue, but the whale remains here for me, sleeping as she has for centuries, singing downwards into the earth, into the deep Atlantic. I could hear her, as I walked along her sleeping back. Her song was not strange to me, I had heard it all these years since I was a small child taken by the hand here, Granny's strong grip guiding me over the land like a rudder, Claire running ahead of us like the wildfire she was, Granny never bothered to scold her, she might as well curse fire for being hot. Always, every summer it was the three of us, while the boys fished for bass in the bay with their grandfather, and our parents stayed locked up in the Esplanade Hotel, sipping tea with the Anglo-Irish, counting the days before we would all go back to the city.

There's somewhere, isn't there, between the bones and the flesh – not quite the mind, not quite the soul, where we keep those feelings we can't bear to have, but there we must keep them, because they make us who we are. Those feelings sent me out to the Old Head today, to where the land breaks into the sky. Dmitri. There are a million things we both need to say. Strange invisible lines sing around us, questions from the past and the present, the unsaid moving between us, decades of conversations we have never had – these bind us together, marry us in a way that is stronger than love. Lord above, do you remember how I felt when no one liked my first novel? When the critics mocked it and the reading public ignored it. And then worse and worse for me, a smear of salt on a weeping wound, they continued to ignore me for some years to come. It wasn't until the love story (you named it for me, remember?) that contracts were organised, photographs were published, cups of tea were offered in dimly lit offices, cheques were in the post. You joked that if I had started with a love story instead of a political critique the acclaim would have arrived much sooner. I hit you, of course. It is almost impossible to write about love, you know that. I argued with you. I said that Shakespeare had invented love for us and we were determined to make ourselves sick on the sweetest parts. And in order to write about love, I had to wade through a quagmire of my own sentimentality. That love story was stripped of easy emotion, a poor woman's Brecht. It made people uneasy, but it was oddly close to the truth of their love, to the strangeness of the experience. So thank God they bought the book. And so many copies.

Not long after, I went into London alone on a book-buying spree. It must have been 1951 or 1952, and I hadn't bought books since, well, forever actually, and I was enjoying myself. At Foyles, I was given a young bookseller for the afternoon, a skinny Clapham lad with flat feet and the shiniest patent-leather shoes I had ever seen. Moving fast for a boy with an awkward gait, he ferried my stacks of books to the disinterested shopgirl who wrapped them up in brown paper and kept a running tally of my purchases on some butcher's paper. I had the books sent home to our London place, except one, which I took with me, wrapped and sealed: Kravchenko's book, *I Chose Freedom.* That was the beginning of my habit of reading in tea rooms. Through reading Kravchenko, Duguet, Buber-Neumann, Ginzburg and Malsagov, I tried to understand what had happened to Viktor, what could have happened to you, to anyone. I have never told you. For all these years, you have thought I liked to go to tea rooms alone.

Today, I stood on this land so close to the sea, feeling the strange seduction of the ocean, the complications of the tides. The day the *Lusitania* was torpedoed the village lifeboat was launched, but the lack of wind meant it took the boys hours and hours to row to the site of the sinking twelve miles off the Old Head. But still our lads joined the Queenstown lifeboat and the ships of the Royal Navy, to save the lucky few, and to bring the bodies back to Queenstown. On my way back to the car I stopped at the small Mary Shrine to pray. You know, don't you, that I don't pray as often as I know Granny would like me too, as often as the women of Munster do, or tell their neighbours that they do. Truth be told, God and I began to have our troubles when I saw those scars on your back. I light candles for Granny in any church I pass and this has tested your patience over the years, my darting into churches of all faiths to do this one ritual, the only ritual I have left. You watch me go down to the Sacred Heart every Sunday, with the whole village, but it must be thirty years since I've been to confession, longer still since I did any decades of the rosary, gave up any damn thing for Lent. And yet my faith is fierce, fiercer still since we have suddenly become older, and we are home for good. But it can't be contained in pages or in walls, and it has appeared out of desperation and fear. So I stood in the wind on the cliffs of the Old Head and surrendered to that. Then I knelt at the feet of the tiny statue of Our Lady and surrendered to Her.

And instead of getting back in the car and

driving home to you, I went up to the old watch-tower, through the long grass there. It was then that I saw her. She was as I have seen her in my dreams, long limbed, blond, and cranky, a long black cat draped over her like a big city stole. 'Hello,' was what she said me. 'Hello,' was what I said back. 'Did you know,' she said as we climbed up towards the watchtower, 'that my father is not a Corkman?' I asked her what of her mother then, and she said oh yes, her mother was from Cork, but Cork city she thought, though she couldn't be sure. She'd never been to Cork city herself, she was too little, but she had heard stories. She unwound the black cat from her neck and popped him down on the ground. He wandered into the watchtower and we followed. She looked even smaller inside the dark tower, like a child of four or five. She held her arms out to me and I scooped her up and sat her on the low sill where she had a view of the ocean, a glimpse of the Head. She looked out to the sea, with a face so fierce I could imagine she was looking out for the French invaders, or the Normans, or the Vikings, she didn't care, she'd fight one or all of them. She had your eyes, blue eyes burnt with white, your jaw (set to laugh or to fight) and the O'Donovan shoulders. The cat purred around my feet.

The little girl told me that the day the *Lusitania* went down a baby was born in the village. (She pronounced *Lusitania* like it was a locomotive from a children's book, 'Loo-see-tane-ya'). I said to her that would be me – I was that baby. I was supposed to be born a Cork city girl, but there you go. The girl stretched her legs out on the sill. I asked her what her name was – the little girl looked at me sharply. 'Do you know what day it is then?' she asked me directly. 'It's Tuesday, my girl,' I said to her, as sharp back. 'My name is Terese,' she said, folding her arms tightly across her chest, as if those were the last words to be spoken in the world. 'But tomorrow I will be Carmel.' I picked up the purring cat and placed him in her lap. He settled there as if he had never left. The girl drew her legs up a little so I could sit on the sill. 'So,' I said to Terese, 'it is a different name for every day of the week then?' The girl nodded, scratching the black cat behind one ear and then the other. 'Tuesday is Terese, Wednesday is Carmel, Thursday is Katherine, Friday is Mary, Saturday is Claire, Sunday is Margaret, Monday is Caithleen.' I asked her where she lived and she replied, 'Here.' I said did she mean in the village or in Ballinspittle and she looked at me as if I were a fool. 'No,' she said slowly, so I would understand her, 'here, in the watchtower.' The toes of her left foot pressed into my leg as I sat beside her.

I told Terese when my grandfather was a young man he'd be up at four a.m. to load his butter cart up with firkins, then drive the rough-and-ready road from the village to Clonakilty; then along the better Bandon Road to the city, to the Butter Exchange in Shandon. This was at least an eight-hour journey, I said to her, if there was good weather and no highwaymen. And when my grandfather was an older man and the railway came to the south-west, then he only had to travel to Rathmore and unload his firkins at the railhead. Then eventually, when the railway finally came right into the village, getting his butter to the Butter Exchange was made easier still. I recalled how my father, looking to life beyond his father's farm, ran to the city when he had grown the legs to take him. It was there he met my mother and married her. He was a butter broker at the Butter Exchange for a good number of years until eventually, with several other men, he went into the creamery at Dunbar Street, just as the Exchange was closing its doors. I was sixteen years of age. Our first butter wrapper featured an Irish wolfhound standing on a little hill, with the words Free Irish State Butter stamped into the earth. Even before the Butter Exchange closed its doors, my grandfather, like most of the farmers out here, had begun to sell to the Barryroe Co-Operative. Terese nodded as I told her the stories of the O'Donovans, she chewed her thumb a little and looked out to the sea. She said to me did I know of one of the old ways with butter, flavoured with wild garlic and unsalted (the cost of salt being what it was), then put in a bog hole and left to ripen. I said yes, my granny told me that was how it used to be done. And more than that, the girl said to me, Saint Brendan and his young monks covered their boat with bovine hides and smeared the hides with butter. I said no, I did not know that, not at all.

She asked me where I lived and I said in the village, in my granny's house, the one she left to my sister Claire and to me. I told the tale of the house. My granny had not lived any of her married life with my grandfather on his farm, and there was much talk of this in their younger years, but eventually both my grandfather and the village became used to the arrangement. There was nothing spiteful or hateful about it. Once the boys were old enough, they could walk or ride to their father's farm when there was work to be done. There was always a Sunday lunch after Mass at the village house, the whole family would be there. Granny knew it was the thought of that house which brought my grandfather closer to the idea of marriage, that without it he would not have given her the time of day, and she meant to keep the house as her own. As much as my father loathed coming back to the village, my mother too, her being from the city, Granny insisted they bring us every summer, she would not stand for anything else. I don't know why my parents did not simply send us into the loving care of our grandmother, we would have been perfectly safe and sound, but mother and father took the same room at the Esplanade Hotel every summer and barely moved from it, being seen occasionally in the church, my father in the pub or my mother on the beach; but mostly in the dining room and front bar of the hotel, taking tea and reading the newspapers, waiting to go home. Claire and I, together with our pack of howling little brothers, filled Granny's house with noise.

'But look at me,' I said to Terese, 'haven't I gone on.' The girl didn't say yes or no to this, she had the most terrible look on her face. I said to her, 'Why don't you come home with me then, my girl? You could bring the cat with you, he would not be a bother.' The girl could not quite get her composure back, but she said nothing, just clutched her black cat tighter, and looked to the Old Head. Eventually she said, 'You best be going, there is heavy rain coming, and there is no shelter here.' She was right, in the time it had taken us to talk a little, the blue sky had been washed out and replaced by a grey sky full of trouble. I got off the sill and placed a hand on her small feet. 'If you ever want to come – just ask for the O'Donovan house above the Coastguard Cottages.' The girl nodded but did not look at me, only through the blasted window, to the trouble coming up from the sea. I left her there, my heart full of her. I sat in the car for the longest time. And the storm rose up and over the Old Head, drenching everything in sight.

Caithleen.

04/12/2011

Hey Lou.

Yesterday morning I woke up at four a.m., nothing to hear except the occasional sleepy driver coming down Vincent Street from a long Friday night in Leederville. It would have been a good time to talk to you, to pick up the phone, but I was waiting on a call from Nate, so I went into the laundry, got on the exercise bike and rode five kilometres into the laundry sink. By the time I finished, Crow Bait was up out of his basket, yawning in the doorway, his left eye gummed up, his tail switching in bloody irritation. 'Sorry, mate,' I said to him. I wiped the bike down with the old Guide Dog Association tea towel, turned on the laundry tap and put my head under the water. A waste, I know, but old habits. I went into the blue-black kitchen, and Crow Bait followed, twirling around my feet like a feather duster. I hit the kettle, opened up the Coronation tin of Irish Breakfast leaf, filled Dad's old work teapot. I could feel the light coming, but not yet. Dad used to say that Perth is only disguised during the night, the dark a flimsy shade over the bloody bright. He'd say give that light half a chance and it's at your door, knocking loudly on the frame. My body rattled from the bike exercise. I poured the tea, left it to brew, let myself lean into those precious minutes, a domestic comfort. As I stood in our kitchen I walked into the side street of another dream, something about a northern Italian city, a piazza, and the Berlotti Brothers. The Berlotti Brothers ran a ladies' hosiery shop, they sold nothing but stockings, beautiful silk stockings from Paris and Milan and Rome. The sign on their shop said, 'Okay! We will return!' and you and I waited on the small balcony. Below in the piazza were tables full of old Italian men, their white shirts grey from decades of cigarettes, but still beautifully pressed by their at-home wives. They sat at tables, bent into them like secretive crows, looking at cards, newspapers, piles of coins. They talked, they murmured, but I couldn't understand what they were saying, they were looking at us, talking, gesturing, dark looks, unfriendly, suspicious. I got angry very quickly, my anger shot up and out of my mouth before I could stop it, I shouted, 'Okay! She's my lover, okay!' and just as the whole piazza was about to rise, scrape their chairs back and come up to have a few words with us about that, the Berlotti Brothers arrived, running along the balcony towards us, saying, 'Scusie, scusie, it's okay, sure, sure, we're a little late but it's okay, sure, sure – Hey! It's okay, they're in love, it's okay.' And they ushered us into the shop and closed the door. I don't know.

I poured the Irish Breakfast into your Penguin mug and took it out to the sunroom. Like the twitch-twitch of a sprinkler head, I could hear our resident willy wagtail out on the back lawn. Crow Bait was already in the room, on the couch washing his paws. I sat down next to him. We watched the light wander its way into the world, walk in like an uncle back from the Second World War; all familiar, day-to-day happiness, you know? I sipped at the tea. Nate's latest postcard was of the Artist and Writers Restaurant, 213 West 40th Street, New York City, *A place where people of diverse talents and different opinions have met for decades to eat and drink in congenial surroundings.* Nate called too, from Park Slope. He's been painting the town, going to Don't Tell Mama, Duplex, the Oak Room, Feinsteins. He's seen Johnny Rodgers, Keli O'Hare, Todd Murray, and the legendary Marilyn Moye. He has been rehearsing during the day with the rest of the performers 'in a bitch of a room in Brooklyn'. Jesse

Luttrell is much, much sexier than he is, but Jesse hates that Nate can sing cabaret in the original German – so one up for the Perth boy. After talking to Nate I took off for Cottesloe. There was a preseason footy match on down in Freo so the train was standing room only. A group of small boys in Dockers jumpers swung around the centre pole and sang, in unison, to every single passenger who came onboard, 'Welcome to the train.' It was sweet, and funny and made the trip one thousand times more pleasant – sunshine, a football match, a Sunday morning, small boys. I got off the train at Cottesloe and walked to the beach. I sat under the Norfolk pines and watched the kids chucking themselves off the Cottesloe Bell and into the sea. We did that as little kids, the boys and I. Nate too, we've watched him many a time throw his body into the air. It seemed to me in that moment to be the only perfect thing to do in an imperfect world. That night I dreamt of a tall, muscular, dark-haired young man who dove through darkness. And the young man dove for so long, and in so many ways, that it looked like he would never reach the water (wherever the water was, I could only see the diving man). And in complete concordance with the logic of dreams, the diver never reached any water at all.

I don't know, these letters were supposed to be about you, and me, they were supposed to be my gift to you, some kind of romantic gesture to let you know how much I still think of you when you're not here, how much I still wish you were here in the middle of the night when the world breaks into my mind like an ugly thief and I need you to get me back to sleep. They were supposed to be a record, a study, a history of our romance, much longer than a decade now, a way to not let time get to what we have, but I have failed, you know? I've wandered, I've digressed, I've chatted to you like a neighbour over the fence, giving you news of this and that, reporting my life like a cheap fill-in column. Perhaps the only thing I have done correctly is find my own faults, punched holes in the thick black walls of my stubborn old beliefs, those strange loops of logic which keep a body moving forward, regardless of the cost to the self and to others. I was going through some old boxes last night, and I found a photograph so old I'd forgotten it. Leighton Beach in the nineties. You and I are standing outside that caravan that used to be up near the highway, the one painted in clouds, the one Annie Lennox steps out of in a Eurythmics video clip. Even with our Ray-Bans on we are holding our hands to our faces, and the shot is an explosion of light, our heads are touching as our bodies lean into each other, and there is only the suggestion of painted clouds and sky behind us, a hint of arms, legs and torsos but mostly we are not there, we are erased by light. This is memory. You walk back to a place you once were, to find someone else there instead.

I remember watching you sleep, watching you dream, wondering what you were dreaming about. It's been one of the reasons I've stayed through the unhappiness, one of the many reasons I stayed, as there was so much love there, in the middle of the night, when nothing else had to be done, or said. It was the perfect time to uncover how much you loved a person, you could feel it, just there, hitting at the wall of your heart like a small butterfly, so delicate you missed it in every other hour. I remember watching you sleep, watching you dream and as I watched you dream I realised that you didn't dream like I did, you dreamt of picking up Nate from footy practice, of taking my trousers to the Vietnamese tailor, of making a roast dinner for the Jameses next door. I realised that you dreamt about shopping lists, about errands to run, running taps, cars that needed a service, bills that needed paying. There was no poetry in your dreams, only practicalities. And I thought, that was probably why we worked, and probably why I still loved you.

Grace.

15th December 2011

Grace. We've just left Andover. Said goodbye to Sharon, Tim and the dogs. We've got Brighton tomorrow night. Stow is asleep. I bought a second-hand copy of *The Human Factor.* It's been so long since I read it that all I remember is my affection for Castle. I've just finished reading the scene where Castle has gone into the Halliday & Son bookshop to request two copies of *War and Peace*. I know he's speaking in code to the bookseller, that the code is a longstanding agreement, but that's all I remember. I am worried about what will happen to him and Sarah. Silly, isn't it? I read your latest letter at Sharon's kitchen table. Your memories are beautiful. I love them. I feel ashamed I can't give you the same. You have made me remember certain things. Things I had forgotten to care about. After lunch (confident no one knew we were around) Tim and Sharon shooed us out of the house. With Stow lying low in the backseat I drove the two of us and the dogs (Fleece and Riley) up to Salisbury Plain. The four of us walked and walked, the weather holding, the wind folding white clouds into a grey sky. The dogs were Wombles on the Plain. They found discarded tennis balls, empty plastic bottles, old chew toys. We walked for a long time, Stow unfolding, relaxing, humming an old Beatles tune 'The Night

Before?' At some point he asked me about the letters I was writing. I found myself talking on as we threw tennis balls for Riley down the long straight chalky tracks. He listened and listened. Just by talking to him I got an inkling, a small understanding of where we were, like seeing a beautiful woman for an instant, then gone. I'm listening to Emmylou on my iPod. 'Wrecking Ball'. Even after all these years it's like smoking the most intoxicating cigarette. There's a point where you just surrender to it, and you don't know if you're going to weep or break up the furniture. This is the one that changed everything for her. So I'm looking for something from it, something as significant. It's the one that cleared away the brick wall she was standing in front of. So maybe things are as simple as that for us. We need a wrecking ball. To clear away what we've surrounded ourselves with. Her voice reaches back and forth across ages, always here and always leaving. If we need this wrecking ball, if this is what's going to work for us, what will it be? I don't know. I'm allergic to therapists, they seem to be cast out of one of two movies: a Woody Allen farce or an Ingmar Bergman tragedy. Neither is very real, very ordinary. I don't pray. We could consult some book or other, some *New York Times* bestseller or something recommended by Oprah. We could talk. Old-fashioned, but it just might work. We really need to be in the same room. I love your letters though. They've changed me the way a good song does. They've let me know things I already knew, but I'd forgotten, forgotten so well I was walking around asleep. We need to meet. In the meantime, give me what you can. Give me words. Lou.

June 22nd '48

David. On June 20th, around eleven o'clock in the morning, I opened the front door to a strange man standing on my doorstep, taking shelter from the drizzle. He carried with him an old-world suitcase, battered and scuffed, thrown from one country to the next, a brown paper parcel strangled by too much string, and a slim black attaché case. There was an absence in the carriage of his body, in the hollow temple of his eyes. He put down his suitcase and held out his hand. He told me his name was Peter de Visser. He asked me if I had received his letters. I told him yes. But I had not replied. He told me he understood my reasons. I said nothing, as I had no compass for what was happening, no proper, rehearsed response. He waited for an invitation into the house. He looked like he would wait all day if necessary. His presence was overwhelming to me. Leaving the front door open, I went inside and made a telephone call.

When I returned, I told him that I had made a reservation for him at the Hinton Firs in Manor Road, on the East Cliff. They would send a taxi around for him. This time of day, it would be no more than ten minutes. He reached into his jacket and took out an open packet of Craven As. He lit a cigarette. He told me that he had something for me. He smoked his cigarette and looked into the hallway of the house through the open door, but said nothing. I asked him if he had walked all the way from the train station and he said yes. When the taxi came, I took his thin black briefcase, opened a rear door and placed it on the back seat. I offered to pay for the taxi but he declined. He said he would telephone the house in the afternoon. Just as the taxi reversed out into the road Viv appeared from the other direction on her bicycle. She leapt off the bike and pushed it up the drive, puffing and panting for effect – really, she's so fit she could have carried the thing on her back. When she reached me, I took the bicycle from her, lightly holding on to the handlebars. 'Why are you standing out here in this soup of a rain?' she said to me. 'Who have I missed just now?' I told her. It had never occurred to me that this, or anything like it, would happen.

Later, that afternoon, Peter de Visser telephoned

the Red Villa. Viv took the call and, Viv being Viv, persuaded him to meet with her. There were other reasons she wanted to do this besides protecting me. As a journalist, how could she stay away, when a witness to the end of the world was sitting in a reasonably priced hotel on the East Cliff? But when they met at his hotel, he said little to her about his experiences. I told Viv that this didn't surprise me. His letters to me had been sparse; as if every word had cost him some unimaginable price. Vivienne told me the item in question was in the thin black briefcase. If I wanted to see it I would have to let him come to the Red Villa, or he and the case would return to Amsterdam. He would wait for my telephone call. When I asked Vivienne how he seemed, what kind of a man, she said if he were a blackmailer (which she doubted very much) he was a lousy one. He seemed considered, she said, yet at the same time ill at ease about the most ordinary things. She thought I should let him come to the house. When she asked me if I had any idea about the contents of the briefcase I answered honestly, I said I had no idea. The next morning I wrote Peter de Visser a brief note and had it delivered to the desk at the Hinton Firs. The note said I was leaving Bournemouth for a few days, but that he would have my answer when I returned. In the meantime, my sister Vivienne was more than happy to show him the sights of Bournemouth. The Bournemouth Symphony Orchestra was giving a concert on the afternoon of June 23rd, and again the evening of the 24th, if he enjoyed such things.

So now, I am at the Forest Park Hotel in Meerut Road, Brockenhurst, the New Forest. King George and Queen Mary visited wounded Indian soldiers at this hotel in 1916, and subsequently named the road in honour of the 7th Indian Division. Several days before D-Day, General Montgomery gave a speech here to American troops from his jeep. I was chatting to a local doctor in the bar tonight. He was one of the few civilian doctors here during the war – surgery four times a day, Lyndhurst and Brockenhurst and back again. With all of the one-way roads and the military checkpoints it was impossible to get around quickly or without wasting precious petrol. He told me that there are few intact remains of the build-up in the New Forest, but there are plenty of war mirages – the hexagon shape of the runways at Beaulieu Aerodome, debris from an Albemarle some miles north of the Stoney Cross, an Army Barrack hut near Fordingbridge, an air raid shelter at Bisterne, some Maycrete buildings, the watchtower of Ibsley Aerodome, the pillbox in the centre of Beaulieu village.

I have OS maps 179 and 180 tacked up on the wall, Bournemouth and The Solent. I walked for five hours today, eight, maybe nine miles? Slow, so slow. I walked north-east from the hotel heading for Black Knowl, where the flat earth rolls out in front of you like a dusty carpet. I walked along the path that cuts a diagonal across the land. Beech and oak were strung out like a green curtain across the horizon. Fat white clouds pressed down on the earth. The wild ponies wandered over the wide open land. I made my way over Bolderford Bridge, past Queen Bower, following the bridlepaths, the lines of beech and of oak. When I came up out of Fletcher's Hill, it was such a sweet, childlike surprise to see Rhinefield Lodge appear as if out of nowhere, as if by some kind of ancient forest magic. I walked back to the village, twilight drawing itself over the land. At the hotel, there was hot water and a deep bath to fill. Any bath has always been too small for me, even when I was a child of twelve, but if it was deep, somehow I always managed to squeeze into it. I took off my walking boots, put them neatly under the bathroom window. I sat down on the cold tiles, my back against the bathroom door and let the tiredness walk its way through my body, drum a rhythm on my skin and through my bones. It was good to feel tired like this, to stretch the muscles, the tendons just slightly, enough to wake them all up out of their stasis. The walk had been a success of sorts, I suppose, it had been done. I rested my head against the back of the door. I closed my eyes. I listened to the sound of the hot water running into the bath. I rested my wrists on my knees, my hands dangling in space to no purpose at all. I could see, in my mind's eye, the unbreakable knot at the centre of my being, my life's work if I wanted it, the thing that could destroy me.

You and I used to take baths at your parents' cottage in Sulz, after hours of walking; your incessant whistling, up mountain and down, I could have strangled you, but you were so happy, what could I do. You would cook recipes of your mother's, and even though the whistling continued I didn't complain, I went to run the bath, to leave you to your childhood kitchen. The water would run, I would test it with my fingers, and the whistling would wind its way into the bathroom and mingle with the sounds of the running water, the hot water hitting the cold porcelain, birds calling out in the forest, the rustle of leaves in the cool afternoon breeze. I would stretch up into the ceiling, stare at the dark wood, the solid beams, the sure architecture of the place. I would think about the wine, which bottle, whether you would smoke after dinner or not, how I preferred to kiss you without the taste of cigarettes on your lips, knowing I would kiss you anyway, I enjoyed you too much.

When the Brockenhurst bath was full, I folded myself into it like a crouching diver, my knees almost touching my ears. I closed my eyes again. I heard you. Vienna. You and I walked in the Prater. The sunlight of a thousand years flirted with the twentieth century. Your watch fell around the good humour of your wrist. The long arc of the day drew a conclusion. The world is simple, but we forget. Among the strollers, the ladies in hats and the gentlemen in suits, there was apprehension, a thin layer of fear in their manner, and gait. You and I were having a small conversation, flirting with one another. You looked at your Longines, looked up at the sun, realised something, but said nothing to me. Back at our apartment you sat on the edge of the bed, still in trousers and shirt, as anxious as a virgin. You drank drowned whisky out of a tumbler and read Rilke. I was naked, in bed, falling asleep waiting for you to say something. Your eyes lingered on my face. Even as I fell asleep I was thinking. Even as I fell asleep problems were being tackled. A white sheet was twisted around my body. My hair was a bloody hurricane. My toenails needed cutting. There was you, me, the bed, the book. You closed the book and slid it under the bed.

You got up and walked around me to the night table. You placed your empty glass there. You picked up my silver case, picked out a cigarette and lit it. You took one drag and then stubbed it out in the already full ashtray. You took off your watch and placed it next to the empty glass. You stared at me with the tenderness of a saint. You eased one knee onto the bed and leant down to kiss me. I asked you in German to unbutton your shirt. You did so. I placed my hands on your chest. As you fell into my embrace, my hands slid around you and came to rest on the pulse of your back. We kissed, two men. I helped you out of your trousers and your underwear. You slid your knees onto my collarbone. I took your penis into my mouth and I sucked on you while you pressed on the wall with the palms of your hands. With both of my hands kneading your arse, I pushed you deeper into my mouth. You breathed like a swimmer, long, deep and measured. Moments before you were about to orgasm I pushed on your chest. You slid out of my mouth still hard. You got off of my shoulders. I looked at you then I rolled over onto my stomach. You pressed the full weight of your body on top of me. You slid into me so easily. You bit my neck as hard as you could. You whispered in my ear. You fucked me until I cried out like a long distance runner hitting his wall. You loved me. I turned onto my back, then pushed you down on the bed, slid on top of you and began to kiss you, my tongue tasting your mouth as if it were sweet toffee. You drew your hands up to my shoulders then ran them down the length of my spine. You began to speak to me, softly, slowly, in German (I had told you, I remember I had told you that the first time we made love German sounded to me like the strangest, familiar music, and it made me ache). I kissed your chest, your stomach, your hips, I placed the palms of my hands on your thighs and ran my tongue along your penis, circling the tip then taking you into my mouth, sucking on you slowly, so slowly I felt as if I were dreaming. I held you in my mouth, then I came up and kissed you, hard. We kissed then, for longer than five minutes, longer than fifteen minutes, perhaps half an hour, we didn't want to stop, there was no reason why we should. You wanted the weight of me, as I was, pressing into you. I could feel the crafted muscle of your legs, your chest, the sculpture of your body. You ran your fingers through my hair, over and over, you kissed my neck, sucked on it like an oyster. I put one strong arm around your back and rolled you on your side. You did not protest. I kissed you, pressed my fingers between your neck and your jawbone like you were delicate crystal being held up to light. When you orgasmed you relaxed in a way I'd never seen before. You seemed to grow into a new skin, into a new self almost immediately. I wanted you to be that way forever. I wanted to keep you there. In between sleeping and dreaming, when nothing is happening, when there is no consolation;

I still want you to leave your fingerprints on my cheekbones, to caress the ruptured skin that gathers like strange needlepoint along my clavicle, to suck all the poison out of my lips, to light a match in the airless chamber of my heart.

June 24th '48

Yesterday, I walked to the village high street. I bought Viv some of the local handmade toys (three ponies and four pigs), and a hand-woven scarf for Mrs Halligan. The village war memorial stands in a little green in Sway Road. The obelisk is still covered in wreaths and flowers from the D-Day Anniversary. I sat on a bench underneath the oak tree that spread itself along the back of the green like a kindly grandfather. The bench was one of two given in memory of a young local lad killed in action. There were ponies across the road, a lucky dip of grey, chestnut, black and beige. A skinny chestnut foal with grey legs was lying down, all stiff-legged and stock still. He looked like a toy that had been pushed over and left there. I sat watching the ponies, with the honoured dead of the village and the oak tree. People walked along Sway Road, hikers with rucksacks, mothers with skipping children, men with folded newspapers. I stayed there for over half an hour.

As in Bournemouth, I waited for some kind of transformation to happen, for some revelation to become apparent, but again, there was only silence. Then for some reason, perhaps simply because I had more time, I began to investigate that silence, to challenge my own assumption that the silence was one of indifference. I sat longer, and longer, trying not to think about anything at all. The oak tree moved. The ponies grazed. People walked past, going about the business of the day. I waited to be struck, and nothing came. I waited to be broken open, and no such thing happened. Something did appear, a thin realisation as fragile as cotton thread. The silence was made up of something, of many things. I sat longer, a little longer still. Something nagged, something pulled. And then it was gone. I was just a man sitting on a bench staring at ponies. I sat a few minutes longer, then walked back to the Forest Park Hotel. Today I made better walking time, eleven miles and eight hours, from the Hotel through Brockenhurst, then along Setley Common to the Ford at Roydon Manor, north to Newlands Copse, Dilton and the Round Hill, then onto Hatchet Moor and Beaulieu Heath, then beyond Hatchet Pond to Beaulieu itself. It's difficult to imagine tank training on Beaulieu Heath, Minka barges on the Beaulieu River, hundreds of warships in The Solent. In the days before the invasion, it was said a man could have walked across to the Isle of Wight. Today, on Beaulieu Heath, there was only purple gorse, butterflies and silence. It was as if the world had been emptied. The wild ponies, those travelling misfits, were elsewhere for most of the day, just one sudden appearance and then gone. They are said to collect for an hour or two out in the open during the hottest part of the day, preferring the heat to the shade of the trees. No one can agree on their origins – descendants of horses from the wrecked ships of the Armada or relations of a small breed of pony brought over by the Romans.

The heath reminded me today of your favourite Paul Klee painting, *Ad Marginem*. It was not typical of his work, but you loved it as a child loves his favourite drawing, with strange, irrational, and fierce love. In the painting a warm red sun sits in the centre of dusty yellow ground while things grow on the borders of the painting, alien plants, curious figures, an upside-down duck. It is not lush, it is mysterious, and of the desert. You found a reproduction of the painting by chance in Vienna – it was hanging in the offices of a lawyer your mother recommended – you offered him a ridiculous amount of money for it and he accepted of course. You came home that day almost laughing with joy you were so happy, and I hadn't seen you that happy in years. We hung the painting, we toasted it with champagne and I spent the night listening to you talk on and on about its beauty, how it had been gifted by Klee to the Russian émigré D.P. Vasilev in celebration of his Dublin wedding day. And even though I was very tired, even though I had a slight headache burrowing its way from one temple to the other, I listened, as there was nothing more magical to me than the sound of your voice, and the happiness there beneath. I may have fallen asleep with my champagne glass in my hand. You may have had to lift me up from my chair and drape me over your shoulders like some sleepy overcoat. I may have mumbled case notes at you while you walked me to our bed. You may have undressed me while I slept on. All of those things may have happened, I won't deny it.

John.

June 25th '48

Dearest David. Late this afternoon Peter de Visser and I walked into the Red Villa. As we walked into the hallway he looked at your paintings, stopping at each, turning from wall to wall, juggling his suitcase and packages like a boy back from boarding school. I could see him reading them, understanding them, even with such quick study. In the drawing room Mrs Halligan fussed over Peter (while shooting daggers at me for not telling her we were having a guest). She took his suitcase and his coat from him and went to ferry them upstairs. Peter placed his other things down on the drawing room table and stepped towards me. We shook hands. I said Mrs Halligan would bring us some tea. He said thank you. We sat down. There was some small talk, I don't remember exactly, blood was pounding in my ears. Mrs Halligan came in with the tea things and set them between us on the side table. She was blushing. Peter, as you know, is very good looking, a real *feschak*. She said to me if that was all she'd be off home and could I still manage, now I had a guest? I told her I could wash up when absolutely necessary, I could even boil an egg if circumstances were dire, not that I'd seen an egg since 1939. She scolded me for my backchat and then wished Peter a pleasant first night (she assumed, though she hadn't been told, that he was staying with us for a while). Was there anything he didn't care for (not that he could expect anything fancy what with the rationing still on). He smiled at Mrs Halligan, then looked over at me for clarification. I explained that Mrs Halligan meant were there any foods he particularly disliked. He apologised for not understanding, and said he liked most food, except vichyssoise, soup he was not very fond of, he hoped this would not be difficult. Peter's concern for her turned Mrs Halligan as red as a beetroot. She assured him his request was no trouble at all. She left us, as Mr Halligan was due any tick of the clock. Peter and I sipped our tea. Soon we could hear Mr Halligan walking up the drive, Mrs Halligan opening the front door.

We sat together, it rained outside, we took our tea *à l'anglais*. We listened to the rain falling over the bones of the house, flicking off the eaves and sluicing through the downpipes. Peter said he had been taking extra English classes since the end of the war, as he had wanted to go to America, to his cousins, his aunt in Brooklyn. But the US refused to allow him into the country, due to his conviction for moral turpitude. Now he was a commercial artist in Amsterdam. He drew advertisements for women's fashions, particularly women's shoes. He impressed with his meticulous nature, his excellent eye, his inventive use of colour. He said he owed his talents to the Bauhaus, without which he would still draw like a schoolboy in the middle of the afternoon. He told me he had something of yours to give me. He told me how you had come to be friends in Flossenbürg. He told me a little about what it was like there. He told me it was a friend of yours in Berlin who had given your name to the Gestapo. He told me that you had asked him to memorise my name.

My address. Daylight was receding, moving down the West Cliff towards the sea, the wide ocean. One of your small paintings hung behind Peter's chair, and he got up to take a closer look at it – *Arc of Joan (1932)*. As he studied the painting he told me a classroom anecdote of Paul Klee's. In 1917, so Klee told it, he was a young clerk at a Bavarian aviation school. He hated what he called his cruel, war-like boots. He used to secretly paint in his desk drawer, and spoke of his art as *andacht zum kleinen* – devotion to small things. Peter told me he had come all this way to see your paintings. I said he was welcome.

I gathered up Peter's brown paper parcel and his attaché case for him. When we got upstairs to his room his suitcase was lying on the end of his bed, his coat was hanging in the open wardrobe. I put the parcel and the case in the bottom of the wardrobe. I told him that the bathroom was down the end of the hall, next to my bedroom. We had coal this week, his room should stay warm through the night. He ran the palm of his right hand over the back of his head. He got his black case out of the wardrobe. He unlocked it. He took out two layers of cardboard lashed together with draughtsman's string. Peter told me that the *Zigeuner Capo* who used to look out for him organised a hiding place for the drawings he did, and for yours also. I took the folio from him. I thanked him, I wished him goodnight and I went back downstairs. The house felt strange, alien, and as I moved through it, passing your paintings at every turn, a force began to gather within me, a soundless grief, as if the meaning of everything were over and gone. I found myself back in the drawing room. The rain had quietly curled into the ocean for the night. There was, as always, the sound of the sea.

Mrs Halligan had turned a single downstairs light on before leaving, knowing I would forget and swear and stumble in the dark. I couldn't sleep. Wouldn't sleep. I sat, downstairs, in the lighted dark. After some hours, I untied the string wrapped around the folio. It contained this single drawing of yours: in this drawing strawberries sat collected in an egg basket. You had drawn out every strand of the basket, like an Old Master, woven it together from old memories of classic renditions. There were hundreds of strawberries, the basket was beautiful but far too big to be collecting strawberries in, and the collector had unwisely placed all the strawberries in the basket. They were beginning to bruise, some of them, some of them were beginning to rot. The basket strands were woven together with browns, and blacks, the strawberries were coloured a thin watery red. Several had fallen out of the basket and were lying on the ground in the mud, almost invisible, covered in grime and dirt. Behind the basket was a small grey road winding up through a small grey village and beyond that was a grey mountain. A figure, a grey man, climbed the path out of the village towards the mountain. He had a tennis racquet in his left hand, I could just make out its old-fashioned wooden grip, the curve of its head, and he was tossing a white tennis ball into the air. The trajectory of the ball was small, too small for a serve, but could do for a groundstroke dug out from the hip. The not-so-young man tossed a white tennis ball skyward. It hung in the air, suspended slightly above his right shoulder.

John.

28th June 1969

Caithleen – When you came home from the Old Head (shaken, tired, pale) I thought you had had an accident, with cattle, or dogs, or horse and cart, but you said no, nothing like that and I could tell by your fear, and your grief, that something strange had happened out there. But I didn't ask. I tried not to worry about you. I slept in the little room downstairs. At dawn the dog came looking for me, nudging my hand with his wet nose, whining to be let out (he didn't want to wake you, but me, that was fine). In the late afternoon you came downstairs and my heart ached to see you. My girl, would you like me to send the dog around to the Old Head? I am so sure that he could coax our young girl home with him. Cat or no cat, he can be quite charming. I want this for your happiness, but I know she wouldn't survive here in the village, the elements are not in place here, the wild air. Has she been here, all these years, waiting for you to come across her in that wild place? It hurts to think of you crying your heart out in that little car of yours, the rain and the tears dissolving everything. The south-west has opened your heart so wide your truest desire has tumbled out onto the earth. You will see her again. She will lead you once again to the watchtower, or some similar place, to sit and talk and share stories. We know that can happen here. It happens in my country too. Along this wild coast, memory conjures. And so be careful. Your love for her in this place has vaulted over thirty years without a second thought. This could happen when I am gone. I could come to you after my death and say to you, look over your shoulder, it's not so far at all, come walk down the road with me.

You confess to me that you have read Russian books in tea rooms. Well, I'm curious, was it my silence that made you believe you had to hide this from me? Or my rage? I am still sorry for that night in the Hi-bar, my fist through the wall. For the party in London, the conservative with the broken ribs, my arrest, the publicity. For those weeks I spent in Clonakilty drinking night and day. I was swinging at ghosts . . . Today I was back with the painting, back with the long white tendrils which crawl across the canvas, which grow out of the white vertebrae cut through the middle of the painting. The rock 'n' roll is very loud now and the dog does not mind. He has developed a kind of immunity to it. The rock 'n' roll underwrites the paint. As I unfurl long lines across the canvas, over the top of the acrylic white ground, mixed methodically with marble grit and pumice, the beat of the band steadies my hand and makes it stronger. Each tendril will take weeks to build, longer still to dry and then to reapply, to rescore. This work, it suits me, the military slowness of art.

The idea for the white painting, it came the morning after my diagnosis. I was downstairs in the kitchen, very early, four-thirty, and the dark black night, it was giving way to a cobalt blue. I was filling the kettle. I was remembering a song from my childhood. The lines fell through my mind so familiar and I began to sing a little, softly under my breath. It made me happy, the day after I found out I was going to die. In my sleepy mind I began to be aware of something – the coolness of the air. There was a cold taste on my tongue, the cool of the hard floor at my feet, the stinging cold of the kettle, all there, all at once. The feeling of the air on my skin was a cool white. And then, for the smallest of seconds, I was thrown back into my childhood, into the real cold, a cold only the poets can accurately describe, that only those born to it can endure; and then it was gone, flying out of the Cork kitchen at a high speed. What I had left, it was a dull, cold taste on my tongue, and the urge to paint.

So here I am, baking in my oven of a greenhouse, drinking pints and pints of water a day, sweating like a poor man on a famine road, swearing like your sister does, boxing with the invisible. These boys I am listening to (what are they but boys, not even thirty), I don't pretend to understand everything they are saying, but I understand their comic desperation. The notorious dog, he is much more old fashioned than me. He still cannot get beyond the sheer noise of the music, its surface irritations. He won't listen for the humour, which I don't understand, when his love for 'The Goons' it is endless. He hopes this is a phase I am going through, and he could be right, I may not listen to this white music again once the white painting is finished. The songs are giving me something. I know I am working three or four days a week, I know I am in my little light box for all hours of daylight, but the work is slow, so slow. It is disappointing and strange that I have left the most difficult painting of my life to the very last. If I live through this, if I manage to steal some more time from God when this is finished, then I will settle down to sketching – the dog walking beside the water counting the ducks, the long-eared owls nesting in the high trees of the woodlands, the lines of cormorants strung out on the sandbanks in the middle of the bay, the grey crows dropping mussel shells onto the village road. I will finally become an Irishman; more than that, a Corkman, who is homesick even at home.

There are things I haven't told you, things I have been afraid to say. You stood there, outside Dr Collins' Clonakilty rooms with my manila folder of tests and you looked defeated. I wanted to apologise but I knew that would only make you angry. You were looking at an enemy you could not win against. I wasn't resigned to death, to my death, but perhaps it has always seemed more natural to me than to you; part of you saw death as an insult to your life, to our life. To me, it is the only reality that gives me the passion I have to live. But you, that day, you wanted to have a fight with Death, to hit him square on his glass jaw and watch him drop to the ground. There was a look of murder in your eyes I had never seen in you, a look that belonged to your sister, not to you. I was frightened. You said to me, clutching the manila folder, almost strangling it, that now I had to do something for you. At that point I would have given you anything you had asked for, you looked like a woman who could destroy Clonakilty with one fierce look, with one terse word. You asked me to write to you. This was not what I was expecting you to say. Like the idiot I am, I was confused. You knew this, and you explained. You wanted me to write to you because you were frightened. There were things between us that had been left unsaid, or forgotten in all of this time together. You wanted love letters.

And I said yes, not knowing what I would say in these letters, or how I would say it. And so this spring we have begun and we will continue through the summer. I will work, you will work, and we will write to one another. Death sits with me and the notorious dog here in this greenhouse. He says nothing, a small man in an un-pressed shirt, unremarkable trousers, tired and unkempt, his socks a sad shade of grey. He drinks great cups of Barry's tea, in no hurry at all. He watches me paint, looking for himself in the work but he doesn't appear and he won't appear. Everyone I have ever loved, here they all are, in this living white. And the line I am working on, the line that runs across the middle of the painting, and through the vertebrae like a white arrow, hot and fast, that is Viktor, the other half of my heart. The dog, he is beginning to work out what it is I am doing, for so long he has believed I have lost the plot, that this painting signals the end of my talent, my vault into nothing, but he has started to stare at the canvas in the same way he has with all of my work these last few years. He begins at the outside left edge of the canvas, where he sits, he stares, he cocks his head at the work, he wags his tail; then he moves on a little, to where he repeats his routine. When he reaches the middle of the painting he walks backwards and away from the canvas until he can see the whole thing, then he sits down, chin on paws to contemplate. He is my best critic.

I have been loved by you in ways I did not expect when we were first married. But I really didn't know you then. I know you now. Sometimes I think I have lied to you all this time, that I have never been honest as I have spent my life running. It has been almost impossible for me to believe that you love me, and so I have kept you at the edges of my heart for all this time. But finally, I have grown tired of my own fear. It has worn away, fallen away, but what a cost there has been to my heart. So if I do not say this to you ever again, if you do not hear this from my lips, then I beg you Caithleen, listen to me now.

This ocean that surrounds us, this vast ocean wandering from here to there along this coast, keeps for me the secret of my life – my absolute love for you from the moment we first met. My shame is that I have struggled with this plain white fact until now. Caithleen, I love you. Now that the painting is well on the way, I can almost see what I have created. With you in my mind, with you at the centre of my body, with you at the centre of my life, it is your name I have carved into the canvas – you are the vertebrae of the white painting.

Dmitri.

27/12/2011

Hey Lou – I've discovered a new café. Cabin Fever in Bon Marché Arcade is petite and homely, warm with pine-clad walls, sixties lamps and creaky wooden tables. Its splendour resides in the rows and rows of pigeonholes flush with tea cups, cups from every decade of the twentieth century, old conversations caught in their lips like historical kisses. Just this week they've set out a dark blue Remington typewriter for the customers, an Envoy III that sits by the window on an old sewing table. A little sign suggests *wanna write a letter to your lover?* (paper and envelopes are fifty cents). One half of a bookend, a ~~kitsh~~ kitsch wooden owl, sits beside the typewriter wondering if I will. At first I didn't want to, not in public, not on a strange typewriter, you know? But as I sat in my lime-green lounge chair sipping soy chai I began to come around to the idea. The typewriter is neat and compact and sturdy and blue, just the right machine to pound out a missive of love. When you strike the keys it's a sound that hasn't been heard in the ~~qorld~~ world for thirty years (we are so far away from a time when typewriters won world wars). When you strike the keys they make a sound like a pistol shot, a sound so definite and sure you feel like a genius, or an ~~orayor~~ orator, or a beat poet. When you strike the keys you just want to keep on fucking writing. You have to wrestle with the thing, like I am doing now, steer it like an old manual car, keep the words together and right and on the page, but the blood and muscle of a typewriter, it is a beautiful thing.

There's a broken promise in these pages, I'm unwinding the words in order to explain something to you.

This love we have, this life we share, I still want it, like you I want to try again, I want to talk and talk, I want to remember whatever it is we have forgotten, but I'm frightened of failing, and the feeling is a little like it was when I came out all those years ago to a soundtrack of The Smiths and Eurythmics. A middle-aged ~~lrs~~ lesbian is supposed to be well adjusted but recently I am young again and uneasy. I was never a natural rebel. This sexuality suits the boundary riders and the misfits and I am neither of those things. When I came out, there

I was with the wild crowd and all I wanted was a steady romance and a good strong cup of tea. So much opportunity to be bad and I squandered it. Perhaps it's only when you have come to this stage of your queer life, the middle, that you realise how fundamental sexuality really is, that it lives beyond the surfaces, beyond the political rhetoric and the street theatre. When you find yourself deeply in love with another woman – well, within that love you find corridors of doubt and fear, a secret homophobia that's strangely familiar.

Oh Christ. This is supposed to be a love letter.

I can see your beautiful face, your dark hair, your neck, the single, definite signature of your back, the playful curve of your arse, those legs. I can see myself beside you, in some bed somewhere, it doesn't matter where, this is you and I together. You're trying to remember a Gillian Welch song. You're singing slow. I'm no help as I have a terrible head for lyrics. There is the afterthought of champagne on my tongue. You reach over to your glass of water and drink deeply. I am nervous. I am always nervous, even after years. You ask me to turn off the overhead light. There is a lamp, which you switch on and shift away from us towards the wall behind. There is no music, no candles, no incense. You hate atmosphere, rebel against it, your only concession to romance is the softer lighting. You are still trying to remember the song. You're sitting up now, your back against the headboard, your eyes closed, you're humming the almost forgotten song, it has hold of you now. I lean in and kiss you softly on the lips, which surprises you, makes you laugh and open your eyes at the same time. You giggle like a teenager and draw me closer to you. We kiss again, deeper this time, without thinking, longer and deeper still. I have one hand on the inside of your right thigh, one hand against the headboard. It's delicate, and tricky, you may shift at any moment, we are both tense, trying not to anticipate or rush anything, pre-empt or pre-judge. We've been here so many times before, we have to work hard at believing we have not ever at all. I like kissing you. I have always liked kissing you. It's how we always begin, but I like it that way. You know I could kiss you for a long time, for as long as you'd let me, but you won't stand for it, you'll be the one to break it off, to demand something else from me a mere second before I am prepared to give it. You push a little on my shoulder with the palm of your hand. We don't stop kissing. I am surprised. But you do, somehow, manage to push me back gently onto the bed, my feet now on one of the fluffy white pillows. That's when this love begins, with the strange and secure fit between our similar bodies.

Love is not what we think it will be, we can't imagine what it will do to us going in, we can't imagine what it will reveal to us, late, in the black blue centre of the night when nothing else is awake, nothing else is alive but our desires. When you are asleep, as I have said before, sometimes when you are asleep I am on the edge of beginning to understand how much I love you because in that early-morning moment there is nothing else to understand. Every other concern is gone, every other motive has disappeared, every other fear is, for now, tucked away in its envelope and I only have one, pure motivation. To be loved. It's a cliché to say that the sleeping lover is beautiful, that the sleeping lover is perfect, but why can't it be true? It's happened, once or twice, when I am not pursued by errant emotions, or too tired to sleep, or wrestling with what I should have said to someone hours before. It has happened that I could see you as you are, without complication. In that is the first impulse of love, its beginning beat. Late last night I had my strangest dream. In my dream, you bore a horrible resemblance to Ulysses. You had acquired the sea-length hair and the ship bones, the old dog and the promise of a bent bow. I was a Penelope who hadn't touched a tapestry for years. You had no words to say to me. You stood there at the entrance to my doorway like you would never leave and never return.

You sent that drunken, romantic letter to me from Berlin, and I loved you for it, and I admired your honesty, your messiness at the end of a long day, your missing me which nothing could make better, that no attempt to reach me, no instant contact or rapid texting could fix. It was honest, and I haven't been very honest. I started these letters as a way to give you something beyond virtual contact, something I thought was more real, more authentic, but I was wrong and I have been lying. There is no honesty in my words. Without you in the room with me everything I say to you is false. I can't give you anything, just words stuck on a piece of paper, pressed into the page with blunt metal keys. Like your emails, sliding off of their platforms, too drunk with what they are trying to say, what they can't say –

This thin piece of paper with its little words is not how I feel about you, it's not what you mean to me, it can't be what I've spent years wandering through, this city of love. Grace.

6th January 2012

Grace.

It's four in the morning in Liverpool. I'm in the Pan Am bar on the Albert Dock. It's rainy, but no snow. The air is clear, stars leap back in time. And I have your love letter, typed on that thin disposable paper, tucked inside the pocket of my Burberry. I could carry it for years, wandering around this city. And no one would ever know its secret. I could have this feeling for years if this night never stopped. I could just feel this happiness. Walking around the city tonight, it seems to me that there is precious little happiness in the world, true happiness. The kind you can grow a real heart with, and protect. To destroy that, to extinguish that small flame in this dark world, well, that is obscene, that is a sin. Every hour we allow this to happen is a century too long. Our happiness has been thwarted not because of some literary obstacle (a missed train, an undelivered letter, a hostile family, an unscrupulous rival), we could deal with any of those things, lord knows you've read all the books, you know all the endings. You are the traveller, Grace. You are the one who has travelled late at night, alone in the rushing dark, without a bloody clue where you would end up. Without money or companionship or safety, shedding your old self like unwanted baggage. I have gone from plane to plane, from year to year, from client to client, the same old me, clocking up the miles, knowing the quickest routes to almost anywhere, but I know nothing, I know nothing. It has taken me almost fifteen years to understand what love is. Today I told Stow I admired his wedding ring. He took it off and handed it to me so I could have a better look at it. The writing curled around it said *Here I Am So Glad You Are.* You can read it several different ways. It depends on where you start. Years ago now, under the pomegranate tree, Patrick told me he liked to stop in Basel, to look at *Ad Marginem*, because it made him remember where he came from. What Patrick saw in that painting was home. Perth. A city carved out of the desert, blooming on the margins, eccentric and a little overlooked, but uniquely itself. A city held together by the deep forest lungs of the south-west, built by the minerals dug up out of the red dirt of the north. A city of cowboys, media barons and billionaires. A city made to leave because it seems so safe and secure. A city to return to when the realities of the world keep you up at night and make you drink just that little too much. A city a little too good for a reputation but so clever, so beautiful it holds many strangers and keeps them longer than they expected to stay. Come to Basel, Grace. Get on a plane. Meet me in front of Patrick's *Ad Marginem.* I want to ask you to marry me.

Lou.

June 29th '48

David – Very early this morning, I went to wake up Peter de Visser. His door was slightly ajar. I pushed it open with the tips of my fingers. He was sleeping on the left-hand side of his bed, on top of the undisturbed bedspread. His jacket, trousers, shirt and tie were laid out next to him. His shoes were on the student desk sitting underneath old newspaper – they had been newly polished. A bare-chested trapeze artist, he slept curled up like a question mark, his right hand cradling the back of his head. I stood there, on the threshold, watching him. Peter de Visser stirred and I took a step back. He sat up quickly. I told him Mrs Halligan was making us all a special breakfast. He smiled and said he would dress. That he wouldn't be long. So while a man dressed in an upstairs room, I descended the stairs. You were four or five steps in front of me, walking down. You were adjusting your braces, straightening your collar, stretching, yawning, cracking your knuckles like a Chicago gangster. You reached behind you to scratch the back of your head. As you hit the foot of the stairs you disappeared.

I grabbed the banister to steady myself. I looked around for some trace of you, a fairytale memento, but there was nothing. I sat on the stairs, not quite halfway up, not quite halfway down. You weren't a ghost. Time had painted you, in a rush but with some technique, like a drunk Duchamp. There had been flecks of brown paint in your blond hair. I'd only seen you in my dreams before. I was glad to only see you in my dreams. Now you were descending my stairs. I wondered if this was what you would do now. I put my head in my hands. I counted to ten, very slowly. Then I counted back down to zero even slower. I opened my eyes. There was nothing to do but go down. Between you and I there were thousands of mornings in front of the bathroom mirror, two men trying to scrub and shave in a space no bigger than a broom cupboard. Two men happy in such close proximity to one another, two men working out a two-step in the glass. Remembering distils thousands of times into a single eighteen–per cent proof event, one neat shot. I ran the flat of my hand from the nape of your neck to the crown of your blond head, teasing you about your barber.

How he fussed over you like a schoolboy, and cut your hair like you were one too. You made a face at me in the mirror while you ran cold water over your comb. You were trying to tame three renegade hairs that never failed to stand at attention, no matter the skill of that attentive barber. Then I began to shave over your shoulder and you swore at me in German, saying why didn't I just wait until you had finished? I could have the mirror all to myself, all to my towering English frame. I laughed at you and said that would be no fun. I couldn't lean into your back like I was doing now. I couldn't kiss your shoulder like I was doing now. You mumbled something into the basin about my degenerate English ways and this was what they taught me at public school. You slapped your face hard with cold, cold water in remembrance of all those freezing Bavarian lakes you dived into as a boy. When you came up from the basin I smiled at you in the mirror, hand towel at the ready like a naked manservant. You scowled at me as you snatched the towel out of my hands and rubbed your face bone dry. This grumbling of yours was what happened in the morning. What always happened between you and I.

Peter de Visser's brown paper parcel turned out to contain a veritable banquet: real eggs, smoked ham and turkey, canned goods, New York coffee, Hershey's chocolate, all sent to him from his

Brooklyn cousins, and carried to us here in Bournemouth. He had brought the parcel downstairs in the middle of the night and when Mrs Halligan arrived and found those unimaginable things sitting on the kitchen counter, she cried with joy. As I came into the drawing room, I could hear Mrs Halligan singing in the kitchen, one of her 'Take me Back to Dear Old Blighty' tunes from 1940, when it seemed Hitler was only a minute away from folding the Southern Shires into his great-coat pocket. Viv had persuaded her to join us when the eggs and ham were ready, had insisted she take some of the chocolate and the coffee home for Mr Halligan. Then Peter de Visser came downstairs. You were nowhere to be seen. We ate together, Vivienne, Mrs Halligan, Peter and I. We weren't prepared for the shock of real food, it was as if we had been eating cardboard for ten years. All of us were totally unprepared for the strange effect a single poached egg would have on us, let alone the taste of freshly fried ham, the sensuality of real coffee.

The happiness we had all expected to wash over us vanished after the second, or third mouthful. What we had dreamt of these years did not bring us our longed-for joy. Eating a real breakfast quietly opened the triple-locked door behind which our desires had lurked and raged and grown strong over the war years. With that door open, and the poor creature exposed to the light, grief was the overriding emotion, casting a grey veil over our sunny morning. So we have something much better for our pains: the memory of the breakfast, a memory that will be of more use to us than the actual event itself. We know how to make such memories last. The wonder of that single egg will be with us all for the rest of the year.

Peter has been in the house for a few days now. We are careful with one another. He is quiet and I am grateful for that. Peter has a little green notebook he has been writing in while he has been here. Inside are detailed notes on your paintings. Peter said yesterday that the Bauhaus may have rejected you; but like the young archer in the *Mahabharata* who is refused by the great warrior Drona, you became the greatest disciple of Klee without ever hearing a single word from his lips. The small green notebook he takes with him everywhere in the Red Villa. He leans against the walls and studies your work, for hours at a time. He sketches, takes notes, chews the end of his pencil, taps the pencil on the side of his head. He is making such a careful study of your work, a *Künstlerroman*. It could be my imagination, some kind of wish fulfilment, but he seems a little better. Mrs Halligan, now she knows the bones of his story, is a little nervous at having him in the house, only because, like the rest of us, she doesn't know how to be in the face of such suffering. At the same time, when she forgets this difficulty, she is quite taken with him.

Today Peter and I travelled to London on the Bournemouth Belle. He wished to see the painting Vickers had borrowed. In the carriage we sat at a small, lighted table, Peter watching the countryside unfold like a well-worn map. The passengers at the other tables burrowed into their newspapers and their Penguin paperbacks; they huddled around the words, the ink, the print, waiting for the world to be remade (whenever that was going to be, an impossible time away). Nostalgia for the war has gone bad, for the most part. You can't live on it, can't feed your children with it, so it's been wrapped up in yesterday's newspaper with the potato peelings. Some children (two small boys) didn't know what to make of Peter and I. Perhaps I was an Officer out of Uniform, or Someone from the Government. Perhaps Peter was Foreign. Perhaps we were former Prisoners of War. Perhaps we were two princes who, having spent their lives locked in a high tower, had suddenly been released into the middle of the twentieth century. We were strange, whatever we were. These two boys (no more than five or six years of age) swept past us, checking to see that we were casting shadows.

Our whispering to one another served no good purpose, it only heightened the curiosity of the small boys as they patrolled the carriage, looking for irregularities. Peter said to me that he didn't know when he could speak at length of what had happened to him, if at all. He said it was like he had experienced a drowning that had gone on for years, a drowning he had eventually escaped, but now he was on dry land, walking and talking again, he had no words for what had happened. Water still coursed through the natural gates and alleys of his body. He could not speak of it. Peter said he still had no idea what happened to Otto, his Berlin boyfriend, he has no idea if he's alive or dead, whether he was arrested, whether he joined the German army or was conscripted, whether he managed to escape Germany and is now having a new life somewhere. Whether or not he survived internment only to be sent to prison to finish his sentence for violating Paragraph 175. In the men of Amsterdam, Peter had seen the gait of Otto, heard his sigh, his laughter, his particular comedy. There he was, his boyfriend, within the bodies of others.

Peter spoke quietly to me, leaning forward in his seat. He looked as if he had told me an amusing travel tale – flying carpets and Arabian princes. My hands twitched like a poker player's at the stale end of the evening, anticipating sudden, swift ruin. I spoke to him. I told Peter you were born in Berlin on the fifteenth of January 1906, the third child, the second boy. You slept badly until the night of your first birthday. As a very small boy you were fascinated by snow, and had to be repeatedly stopped from burrowing holes and burying yourself in snowdrifts. While your mother shopped in the Old West district, you (at seven) learnt to skate on the ice rinks by watching the couples there. In second year at the gymnasium you developed the bad habit of solving arguments with your fists, a habit which would have persisted had your older brother not boxed your ears to stop it. You hated athletics, but loved to swim. You ran one hot summer afternoon from home to an ice-cream parlour half a mile away after the captain of the swimming team had telephoned your house, saying he wanted to talk about your butterfly stroke. You only took up drawing when a serious ear infection stopped the daily trips to the gymnasium pool. You pretended to be drunk so as to be affectionate with your friends. You took in the *Berliner Luft* at the Eldorado, the Silhouette, the Kleist-Kasino. You loved Berlin, were indifferent to Munich, and prayed to live in Vienna. You decided to become an artist on your nineteenth birthday. Your application to the Bauhaus in 1928 was roundly rejected. You wrote to Paul Klee in protest – and made yourself famous for a day by pitching a tent in front of the Masters' Houses and sleeping overnight. In 1929, frustrated and thwarted by this persistence with art and your rejection of commerce, your father sent you to England to meet in a North London Hotel with the manufacturers of the finest Manchester linen. While there, drinking into the early morning at Malcolm's, you slipped, fell and hit your head on the corner of a table. Some of your new-found English friends hauled you to your feet and threw you in a taxi, imploring the driver to take you 'round to Barts, just to be sure. When the weary night doctor there pronounced you as nothing more than drunk but sobering up (no concussion), you left with the day's fresh newspaper, a packet of new cigarettes and a small box of aspirin tablets. On the stairs of Barts, with a military band hammering your skull, you saw me.

These things I told Peter.

I told him about the Longines watch I gave to you for your thirtieth birthday. How I ran through the rain with the watch buried deep in my overcoat, ran to our tiny Rummelhardtgasse apartment with its Napoleonic bed and stacks and stacks of canvas. Exhausted after work, I leant against a wall, in the one slim space without canvas. My eyes closed slowly, feeling like exotic hothouse flowers. My arms folded as if I were a solider on leave. I wanted to sleep, so I did sleep, standing up. I slept like this for half an hour, then I drank tea, I watched you work. You told me painting was working the world out. It was diving into cold, clear mountain water. Crying in the night without dreaming. Ducking a fist in the face. It was boxes of old love letters. Leaflets strewn on the streets like yellow flowers. Suitcases stacked at train stations. These things I whispered to Peter, while the fine muslin cloth that embalms me in the world unravelled itself, like so many used bandages, into an untidy mess at my feet. There was no comment from the carriage. No stares of shock from the ladies. No butcher-hook looks from the gentlemen. The train travelled on without incident.

I remember. You kissed me, when I slipped the watch into your trouser pocket. And from that day forward you wore the watch while you worked. I remember those scratches on the face that I warned you would happen, the soft underbelly of the leather strap. You painted (you said) to understand the absence of love, the absence of God, to know the glorious and terrible nothing at the centre of everything. You worked as hard as the faithful, as hard as those who had their belief secure in their scrubbed souls, as hard as any one of them. You had the paint, and the mute white canvas, and your love for me, so powerful, so tangible you swore you could have torn great sheaves of it from the air. You had these things. No great words, no holy books, no histories of faith. Only the mind that you had and the heart you had opened. I remember.

This morning, on the train, Peter stretched his arms up towards the ceiling, waving his hands like Al Jolson. It was then that I noticed he wasn't wearing a watch. I realised that I had not seen him wearing one since he came to Bournemouth. Peter grimaced and nodded to something behind me. I thought I had imagined that someone was breathing quite close to me. I turned around. Standing behind my seat, but peering around it were the two small boys, breathing in unison like small dragons, their nostrils flared, their eyes bulging. It occurred to me at that moment that they were twins. Then, from the small boy closest to me, the interrogation began. Where were we going (London). Where had we been (Bournemouth). Where were our wives (we had no wives). Where was home (Bournemouth for me, Amsterdam for my friend). Was Amsterdam in America (no). Was he an American, he looked American (no). Was I sure, he looked like a gangster (yes, I was sure). Why were we whispering (we didn't want to disturb anyone else). What were we whispering about (where we would like to go for lunch). Were we spies, we looked like spies (no, we weren't spies). What did I do in the war (I was a doctor). Why didn't we have wives (we were unlucky in love). The other small boy disappeared from my view, and then he began to kick the back of my seat, quite hard. The interrogator whispered to me that his brother was a bully, didn't I know, and there, he could whisper too if he wanted to. He doubted that his brother could whisper, didn't I know, as he was always yelling his head off. And with that he kicked his brother in the shins, which caused both of them to bounce off one another and into the aisle, rolling and giggling like two small bear cubs. As the volume and pitch of their mother's voice increased, so did the ferocity of their wrestling. It was obvious there was no father in attendance, so Peter rose from his seat and stepped into the melee. Grabbing both boys by their pants, he swung them like tiny sides of beef then set them on their feet, swaying. He leant down into their little faces and said, in his best Chicago accent, 'Waddaya think youse guys are up to, huh? Where do you think you are – a bowling alley? Why, I oughta roll you two down this aisle like a coupla bowlin' balls!' The brothers squeaked, turned and ran up the aisle and into the arms of their mother, who smiled her thanks. Peter nodded, walked back towards me, and sat down. He was almost laughing. I felt something so unfamiliar it took me some time to recognise it – happiness, there. A lit match and then gone, but unmistakably, there.

At Waterloo, Peter and I met Carter and Lawrence. They are older, tougher and leaner than you would remember, everything unnecessary in them burnt away by a war spent working in field hospitals. But they still looked like a recruitment poster for Empire. We have seen each other quite a lot since that first day of my return, but it remains difficult, for all three of us, without you. Carter and Lawrence both still practise, but (to be discreet) in different areas – Carter flitting between St Mary's and St Giles, Lawrence specialising at a Harley Street address. We don't talk medicine anymore, only if Lawrence calls me, begging for my advice. Carter jokes that I am still Lawrence's favourite medical textbook. Carter and Lawrence were good with Peter. Kind. Not too familiar, not too polite.

We found refuge from the unusual heat in a basement restaurant I had never heard of, though Carter swore he'd been dining there since the early twenties. We were early for lunch. Waiting for alcohol was difficult for Carter and Lawrence, but they had no choice. We all sat there with glasses of tepid water, reading the menus like we were studying Ovid, waiting for service to begin. I looked at Peter's hands, lightly holding his menu as if it were a precious thing, as delicate as origami. He was studying the design, the layout, the text, wondering at its absolute lack of innovation, its bold stab at blandness. He was redesigning it in his mind. I doubted if he was even reading the words. When it came time to order, he would falter, and have to ask for more time. I found there was something oppressive about the murky downstairs light, as if it were stuck in the nineteenth century, and struggling even to enter the room. I felt like we were sitting in the bottom of a black, upturned top hat. I found it difficult to breathe. My left eye closed and opened like the peephole of a West End club, repeating the movement too many times over a matter of minutes. No one noticed. Peter was still shaking his head at the menu typeface, Carter and Lawrence were having a serious discussion about the believability of the steak-and-kidney pie. It was wrong, having Peter seated next to me. It was right. It was horrible.

I began to believe that the restaurant walls were dripping with condensation, that the temperature in the room was sliding towards uncomfortably cold, that there was no food to be ordered, no waiters to take our order, no kitchen, no service of any kind, that all this was an elaborate joke to get the four of us into the basement. I asked Carter for a cigarette. Carter looked at Lawrence. Lawrence looked at Carter. 'You don't smoke,' Carter said to me, 'you haven't for years.' I said I understood that, but would he mind. He replied, 'No, of course not. Lawrence, give the man a cigarette.' Lawrence sighed, shrugged like a drummer, took his cigarette case from the table, opened it and presented it to me. I took a cigarette, and then his lighter. As I inhaled, the room became warmer, friendlier. Peter pressed his shoulder to mine and asked me to explain several of the dishes on the menu, he had no clue as to what they actually were. I began to underline the mysterious items with my cigarette hand, explaining their origins, and their appeal to those raised by King and Country. These items explained to Peter, I delicately shifted my weight away from him, turned my head away from his and took another drag on my cigarette. Everything tasted of ashes.

Peter and I arrived outside Vickers' rooms almost exactly on time. Vickers was in the street, standing by a running motor, leaning into the open driver window, his head nodding like a sprung jack-in-the-box. I guessed he was farewelling his last client, who was obviously in need of some delicate reassurance. Vickers saw the patient off with a strong, purposeful wave and then, observing us, strode across. He shook my hand, then Peter's, and motioned for us to follow him into the building and up to his rooms. We didn't engage in small talk on the way up, we turned through the stairs together without speaking, catching occasional glimpses through slotted windows of the small, manicured garden behind Vickers' building. At the first turning of the first stair, I saw two men, an older man and a young lad, standing under a yew tree, the older man leaning on a shovel, the young man leaning on the tree itself, the flat of his hand pressed against its trunk in a friendly way. At the second turning of the second stair I heard the lad laugh, and then the very faint but unmistakable sound of the older man's voice (not unlike my father's, very like my grandfather's), his voice the sound of seawater pounding Bournemouth rocks. As we climbed away from these men, and through the third turning of the third stair, I felt an immense, inconceivable sadness, as if I were actually leaving my father and my grandfather, as if by climbing these stairs, leaving them behind, I was never to exist. That young man standing by the yew tree would never become my father, that old man with him, never my grandfather. When we reached Vickers' rooms I felt disturbed, disorientated. Vickers conferred with his secretary about a later appointment, then motioned for Peter and I to follow him into his room.

Peter and I sat in Vickers' too-comfortable chairs. He offered us tea, which we both declined. Peter looked at your painting hanging on the wall, the one that Vickers had taken on loan from me. I said to Peter, the painting is called *Flitterwochen*. Honeymoon. Peter got up from his seat and walked over to the painting. I told him that you had painted it drunk, in our apartment, in the early hours of the morning, a few days after the *Anschluss*. You were enraged while you worked. As we all looked at the painting (Peter, Vickers and I), I remembered that often then after hours and hours of painting through the night, you'd come to bed naked, sweating, drunk on vodka, then you'd wake me up and kiss me – no tenderness, none of your usual finesse – short and sharp. You would snap to sleep after that, snorting and snoring. I would lie awake with you in my arms, and I could still see the monster you were creating; an exploding, molten, orange sun, strangled by rivers of red fire, torn open and thrown across the solar system by a furious God, spinning, dying and collapsing in a corner of the universe blacker than black, where no stars bled their ancient light, not a single one. Peter said, 'Klee believed the artist is more than an improved camera; he is more complex, richer and wider. He is a creature of the earth, and a creature within the whole, that is to say, a creature on a star among stars.'

I thought I could hear the sound of wood being chopped in the garden below, until that was all I could hear, the sound of an axe working its way through wood, the rhythm of the sound, its sure repetition, and there was my grandfather, unable to face me, his back to me, looking out of Vickers' window and into the street below. I could smell his pipe, the polish on his shoes. And there was my father, leaning over Vickers' desk, sorting through Vickers' messy case notes, burdened with worry, organising the papers into some careful order. I sat in my chair, not knowing what to think. I could see Peter's hands, painter's hands, but not as delicate as yours, more like those of a carpenter. That last evening as I walked up the stairs to our Rummelhardtgasse apartment I noted the time, eight-seventeen – a meaningless time, a nothing time. As I stepped out onto our floor I saw that the door to our apartment was wide open. It had been flung open. My chest tightened. I felt lightheaded. I stood in the doorway. The white chiffon curtains were open and all of the lamps were switched on. I walked into our bedroom. The white sheets on our bed were pulled back, the pillows were in the centre of the bed. Your clothes, your shoes, your suitcase were still there, but your passport, your papers had gone. Your Longines was sitting on the nightstand. I sat down on the bed. My heart fell into a much slower time.

June 30th '48

Dearest David,

Peter left Bournemouth for London this morning. He is going up to the museums, the galleries, for a week perhaps, then Southampton and home to Amsterdam. He gave me a note before he left, asking me to read it once he was gone. As he was leaving, Mrs Halligan kissed him on the cheek, I shook his hand. He left with *Arc of Joan* carefully wrapped and placed in his thin black briefcase. He tried to refuse this gift but I insisted. Vivienne embraced him then quickly departed for the conservatory. She needed to be alone. She misses you every day, she never tells me so, but I know it to be true. This afternoon at 3 p.m. there was a BSO concert in the new Winter Gardens. Even though they were playing Mother's beloved Beethoven, I persuaded Vivienne to come with me. The program was Brahms Academic festival Overture; Sibelius Karelia Suite; Beethoven Piano Concerto No. 4; Borodin Polovtsian Dances; and the first public performance of Gordon Jacob Symphony No. 2. The conductor was Rudolf Schwarz. At Auschwitz they'd broken his shoulder blade, and as he dipped into the waters of the music, drawing the sounds up for the audience to marvel at, you could see the damage in his body, the slight stammer in his movements, the wrong punctuation.

As I listened to the music I took out the note that Peter had left for me. He may come again next summer. Before he left for London, Peter told me that he remembers standing in the dark, in the long blue dark, lining up for the first time in the Flossenbürg parade ground with the other men: The men must sew their prisoner numbers and pink triangles onto their prison clothing. The pink triangle, with the prison number just below, is to be stitched into the left breast of their jackets and coats as well as on the outside right trouser leg. The pink triangle is a few inches larger than any of the other triangles in the camp so that the 175ers can be seen clearly from a distance. The *Capo* calls out two names at a time. One man takes the pieces of cloth, and another the needle and thread. Peter is paired with you. Peter takes the needle and thread and sews the pink triangle to your jacket.

This line of communication between you and I, this thin grey line between us, seems to me at times the most absurd piece of artifice, and at others the greatest, simplest way to remember you. I am worried that without it I could wander into myself in such a way that I will never find my way out again.

There's a line your brush would follow after weeks of preparation, after weeks of layering paint on paint to create the right language on the canvas. This line would be the melody of the piece, the notes that linger over the top of a rich arrangement, and it would come to you as clearly and as easily as a revelation. After months of sketches and weeks of working with the canvas, this line would be the soul of the work, wandering over the top of everything like a beautiful lone bird over a blood and earth landscape.

Here is my line, David, the line of these letters. Tonight I can see your blue eyes again, the clearest blue, the deepest blue. I stayed there for the longest nights, in the night blue of your eyes, I curled myself into the smallest corner of your beautiful eye and slept, for a thousand years it seemed, and needed nothing, no rest, no dreaming, no comfort, only the blue, to be totally surrounded, by blue, and you. I can see your eyelashes, like words unspoken, your eyelids, perfect like Rilke's poems, I can see your smile, curled like a secret kiss, your lips, blooming, your cheekbones sculptured, your skin the canvas upon which all this beauty rests. I think about you and I know this much to be true. I love you no more or no less, I need you no more or no less, I desire you no more or no less than I did those years in Vienna, those moments in London and those minutes in Bournemouth. No one is simply given a love like this, it is not a common gift, it is grace. So I remember your love, through the eye of these words, through this disintegrating heart of mine.

John.

Acknowledgments

Letters to the End of Love is a work of fiction. The characters and most of the circumstances depicted are imagined. However, certain historical events within the novel required a significant amount of research, and I have many people to thank for their help and assistance. Dr Klaus Müller, world expert on the Nazi persecution of homosexual men, helped me greatly with the very difficult task of writing a fictional Holocaust story and encouraged me to continue when the task seemed too difficult.

During my visit to County Cork in 2010 I was fortunate enough to meet the Irish writer Damien Enright and his lovely wife Marie. Damien was gracious enough to answer my questions about the south-west of Cork and to share some of his stories about a landscape he has lived and worked in for over twenty years. My thanks also to Peter Walstenholme, who shared with me his experiences of coming to Ireland in the late 1960s. And to Noel Fleming and Billy Fleming at the Anchor Bar in Courtmacsherry, thank you for your memories of village life and for your unsurpassed hospitality. My thanks also to John Walker, for sharing his knowledge of Bournemouth during World War Two, for allowing me to take back to Australia a precious copy of his own personal recollections, and for his comments on the final draft of the Bournemouth story.

I am also indebted to the following people and organisations: Anja Fritz at the Flossenbürg Archives for providing me with several personal histories of homosexual prisoners at Flossenbürg concentration camp; the Jewish Holocaust Centre, Melbourne; the United States Holocaust Memorial Museum; staff at the Sheffield Archives for their help with the Edward Carpenter Collection; Peter Kazmierczak at Bournemouth Library; Val Davies from the Bournemouth Local Studies Group for our cup of tea at the Russell-Coates Art Gallery and Museum; Carolyn Butterworth from the Bournemouth Music Library for answering my questions about BSO concerts in the 1940s; Peter Basham for his advice on London teaching hospitals in the 1920s; Steve Jebson at the Met Office in Devon for a rundown on the weather in Bournemouth in June 1948; David Lawrence (president and founder of the Southern E.

Group) and the National Railway Museum (UK) for their advice on the Bournemouth Belle; Karen Watson at the Mass Observation Archive, University of Sussex; Jennifer Healy at MindtheGapFilms for kindly sending me a copy of the documentary *Anne Madden: Painter and Muse*; Anne Madden herself for her kind correspondence; Brigitte Murphy at RTÉ for clearing up The Goons question; the staff at the Cork Butter Museum; and, finally, Dr Nina Zimmer at the Kunstmuseum Basel for advice on Paul Klee's *Ad Marginem*.

I am also indebted to the following works: *Conditions of Love: the Philosophy of Intimacy* by John Armstrong, *Berlin Childhood around 1900* by Walter Benjamin, *Auschwitz and After* by Charlotte Delbo, *A Terrible Splendor* by Jon Marshall Fisher, *Code Name 'Mary': Memoirs of an American Woman in the Austrian Underground* by Muriel Gardiner, *The Men with the Pink Triangle* by Heinz Heiger, *Prisoners of Fear* by Ella Lingens-Reiner, *The Pink Triangle* by Richard Plant, *I, Pierre Seel, Deported Homosexual* by Pierre Seel, *Bent* by Martin Sherman, *Goodbye to Berlin* by Christopher Isherwood, *Maurice* by E.M. Forster, *Four Quartets* by T.S. Eliot, *The Thinking Eye: The Notebooks of Paul Klee, Volume One* by Paul Klee, *The Diaries of Paul Klee (1898–1918)* by Paul Klee, *Early Irish Farming* by Fergus Kelly, *The Farm by Lough Gur* by Mary Carbery, *A Place Near Heaven* by Damien Enright, *Eating*

Scenery: West Cork, the People and the Place by Alannah Hopkin, *The New Forest at War* by John Leete, *Gulag: A History* by Anne Applebaum, *Hope Abandoned* by Nadezhda Mandelstam, *Hope Against Hope* by Nadezhda Mandelstam, *Kolyma Tales* by Varlam Shalamov, *The KGB's Literary Archive* by Vitaly Shentalinsky, *The Whisperers: Private Life in Stalin's Russia* by Orlando Figes, *The Gulag Archipelago 1918–1956* by Aleksandr Solzhenitsyn, *Alexander Dolgun's Story: An American in the Gulag* by Alexander Dolgun and Patrick Watson, *Alexander Solzhenitsyn: A Century in His Life* by D.M. Thomas.

Grace's journey imagery was inspired by the article '5 Reasons to Get Cancer' by John Tarrant (particularly Reason 3). You can read the full article at http://tarrantworks.com.

My profound thanks to Madonna Duffy at UQP for her faith in my work – I could not have asked for a more enthusiastic and dedicated publisher. My thanks also to Rebecca Roberts, senior editor at UQP, for keeping me and the manuscript on track. To my wonderful editor, Judith Lukin-Amundsen, for her generous and wise attention to the manuscript. To Allison Colpoys for the cover design of my dreams. And to my agent, Sheila Drummond, for her advice and guidance.

I am deeply indebted to Julienne van Loon, whose mentorship has sustained me through the lengthy writing process. Thanks also to Ann McGuire for her keen insights, and to Deborah Hunn, Carol Major and Caroline Jestaz for their expert opinions. My thanks also to Curtin University in Western Australia, and to Varuna, the Writers' House for my time there in 2009 and again in 2012.

Thank you also to Trent Baker, Geoff Buss, Brooke Davis, Sandy Foy, Maureen and John Gibbons, Carmel Jackson, Clayton Jackson, Natalie Kon-yu, Shelley Dylan Lewis, Brigid Lowry, Aquila McKenzie, Ian Nichols, Kristina Olsson, Christopher, Bronwyn and Annabel Read, Tor Sagrabb, the staff and regular customers at Collins Booksellers Cottesloe, all the Sadler clan, the Silver Spoon Society, Lyn Talmont, Lencie Wenden and Brenda Walker.

And, finally, my greatest thanks go to my wife, Melanie Rodriga – for her continued faith in the novel; and for her patience, compassion, humour and love.